My Demon World

The Constant Battle in a Young Man's Mind

Divon Delgado

ISBN# 978-0-692-76128-1

First Edition
For information about wholesale orders, please contact:
DIVONVILLE BOOKS at www.divonville.com

Author: Divon Delgado
1st Editor: Nadine Joy
2nd Editor: Anne Violette
Cover Designer: Anne Violette
Manufactured in the USA

Dedication

This book is dedicated on a personal note to my angel Grandmother Mary Grajeda Daywood. Days after your passing I went into a dark place and needed to release to go back into light. It broke my heart to lose you and will cherish those special memories we had together. The journey I went through in my mourning period gave me the strength to successfully start and complete writing this book. I love and miss you every day. I know you are looking down at me and smiling with your open arms. I love you Grandma Mary.

Sincerely,
Your Grandson

Divon Delgado

Author/Artist

Table of Contents

Chapter Eleven

Chapter Twelve

Chapter Thirteen

About the Author

Introduction

Schizophrenia is a mental disorder that affects people all around the world. Many individuals do not realize they suffer with this mental illness. Having close friends who have dealt with this disorder, I became interested to learn more about the signs and symptoms. Upon further study and research, some characteristics of Schizophrenia are more noticeable than others.

The following book is a work of fiction based upon some noticeable traits that I derived from many mediums, including books, articles, TV, the Internet, and in talking to physicians and patients dealing with this illness. Some of the qualities found in schizophrenic patients include:

- Disorganized speech- they usually talk without making any sense.
- Negative symptoms-lack of interest or motivation of everyday things.
- Delusions-beliefs that is not true about being in danger or having special powers.

- Bizarre behavior-weird acts by individual
- Hallucinations- the five basic senses in our human body being used (hearing, sight, smell, taste, and touch) but they are often imagining using these senses.

There are medicine for this disorder and common treatment. You can find many different mental disorder support groups and blogs on this subject for help and advice. Unfortunately this illness does not ever go really away. Are deadly or severe harmful acts to self or others if left untreated?

Chapter ONE

WHAT HAPPENED TO ME?

It was a dark, cold and windy night. A young man crawled out of a dumpster in a dark alley; badly beaten. His clothes were ripped, with fresh blood stains all over them. He was unsure how long he had been unconscious, but he looked around, trying to comprehend what happened. Nearby, a stray dog gobbled down some food that did not make it into the dumpster.

The young man's name was Kris. He was about 5'5 tall, Hispanic, and very fragile. His unhealthy, thin frame barely weighed about 117 lbs. His eyes were dark black to match his short, black hair. He tried to get up, but his body was in excruciating pain. He moaned and cried, as he slowly picked himself up, one arm and leg at a time. Everything was in slow motion. At that rate, it felt as though it would take forever to get anywhere by the way his body barely moved. Then, Kris began to have flashbacks of what happened.

I first met Ian at a carnival. He was a handsome guy in his late twenties, with dirty blonde, short, clean-cut hair. His eyes were like the color of sky blue. He stood about 5'11" and weighed 175 lbs., with a light complexion. One could not help but to notice his nice skin tone, having derived from a beautiful, African American mother and Caucasian father. Ian was poised, well-mannered and educated, which I discovered throughout the two months after meeting him.

Initially, I had gone to the carnival alone. While walking around and enjoying the lights and people-watching on the rides, I felt a pang of hunger. I reached deep into my front pocket to find some loose ones; at least enough to buy a hot dog and a bottle of water. As usual, I did not have much money on me. But the hunger overtook my desire to save what little money I had left.

As I started pulling dollars out, some of the coins fell down to the ground. This was the very moment when I first laid eyes on Ian.

Noticing my dilemma, he came over to help me pick up all the coins. I thought he was the sweetest dreamy gentleman. Not many people would have stopped to help. Ian looked at me inquisitively.

"Who are you here with?" he asked.

"I am here alone," I replied. "Thanks for helping me."

"No problem," he grinned.

"Say, do you want to join me?" I asked boldly. "I do not have much money, but I can buy two hot dogs and give one to you."

Oddly enough, Ian responded favorably. "Sure, why not? I am also here alone. I was supposed to come with a group of friends because it is the last weekend of the carnival here in San Antonio. But they all flaked out on me." He shrugged.

"What a bummer. Well, at least now you got me."

After waiting in line and making small talk, we finally got the hot dogs. Instead of buying bottled water, I requested free cups of water so that we would both have some. The hot dog was pretty good, or maybe I was just really hungry.

After eating, Ian and I just strolled around the carnival. There were a lot of happy families and couples walking throughout the grounds. The annual San Antonio carnival was a local favorite, with many different rides for both kids and grownups. The aroma of popcorn, grilled chicken, turkey legs and other yummy foods filled the air. It was a very pleasant scent.

My new companion and I talked a little about ourselves

and shared a few details about one another's lives. Nothing too overwhelming or personal. I made sure of that. After that night, we stayed in contact and became friends. We texted every so often and hung out sometimes.

Two months after meeting for the first time, Ian and I decided to go out to a local dance club. It was very dark and surreal. The smoke fog machine, laser lights and hundreds of guests filled the club with energy. We drank for a couple of hours.

Alcohol has a way of muddling things. Little did I know right then, but things were about to go awry.

There was a guy that seemed not to like me and started staring at me intentionally. Then, I saw him whispering to someone about me, which I could tell by his body language and facial expressions. I felt hate gathering up inside of me. Perhaps he was making jokes because of what I looked like or what I was wearing. The alcohol gave me the bravery to face bullies in whom I would never have mustered the courage to face before. I went right up to the guy and pushed him.

"Who do you think you are, talking about me?" I yelled into his face. Suddenly, the guy disappeared. All I saw in front of me was a broken mirror on the club's wall. Where did that guy go? It was unbelievable.

Then in the blink of an eye, I felt four arms grabbing me and shoving me out the door. It was the two bouncers, like trolls guarding a bridge.

Everything went dark from that point on. I heard people

talking from a distance, but I could not return any response. I barely understood what they were saying. Others near me panicked. My body started shaking with fear and I became distraught. My anxiety level increased.

Why couldn't I wake up? Was I still alive or dead?

I started scratching my head like someone who has a rash. First slowly, then faster. As I ran my hands over my head, panic rose through me. Minutes later, I checked to see what I had left in my pants. Pocket after pocket I searched, to no avail. I realized everything was gone. My wallet, I.D, credit cards and money were all missing; even my cell phone.

"What am I going to do now?" I wondered out loud. Where was my friend? How did I get here? As I stood in the empty alley, I was dazed and confused.

I looked at my wrist and noticed a hospital name band. It had my real full name on it. When had I been in the hospital?

I stumbled down the alley to the main street to find some help. As I walked, I started reflecting on the past years of my life. There were so many things I had conquered and lived through. The pain mixed with occasional happiness; in between the chaos within my mind. I saw the infinity of space or formless matter. Visions were supposed to have preceded the existence that was wrapped within my Universe.

A flashback of being at my cousin Bree's apartment came out of nowhere. She was immersed in a local city girl gang. Bree was a tough young girl, despite her innocent and sweet appearance. Ironically, she would not hurt a fly. Bree was 5'8" tall, 135 lbs. with an athletic build, and dark, jet black, curly, kinky long hair that reached past the middle of her back. She had an olive skin tone, honey brown eyes, perfect smile, and deep dimples on each cheek. Her looks and body were the total beautiful package. Her nickname was "dimples".

Although Bree was tough now, she was not born that way. Since moving into the projects – a low housing assistance program – two years ago, she either had to fight or get beat up. Of course, Bree fought. She lost sometimes, but quickly learned to win all thereafter. That is when she entered the gang world.

In school, Bree was liked and feared at the same time. We went to the same school, but Bree was a grade behind me, even though we were only four months apart. Although she was very smart, Bree did not put much effort into making good grades in high school. I felt it was an honor to be around her. Even though I was a bit older than Bree, we hung out together with her friends. It was cool at the time.

One day, we were all chillin' at Bree's place. I had a major headache. I asked someone for an aspirin, but instead they gave me four little blue pills. I swallowed them anyway.

Only minutes later, I heard a gunshot and it nearly startled me out of my skin. In my haste to get away, I jumped over a wall. I somehow ended up on the swing set of a playground. When I looked at my hands, they had snakes crawling all over them. I was screaming, trying to shake them off. The snakes were crushing my fingers and hands. My hands were so heavy and I was shaking badly. I saw blood dripping from my fingers from the snake bites.

Suddenly, someone grabbed me from behind. Without looking to see who it was, I took them by the hair and started bashing their head on the side walls of a brick building. I heard people screaming, but to me it was just background noise. I was focused and intent on beating the shit out of this mother fucker who grabbed me.

Then, a bunch of random guys started yanking on my arms and legs to calm me down. I blacked out. When I woke up, I was in the hospital.

"Don't worry, she's going to be okay," said a nurse.

"Who?" I asked, not fully understand what happened.

"Your cousin, Bree. You nearly killed her. But don't worry, she told the personnel that she was jumped and assaulted by three girls that she had never seen before. She did it to protect you," the nurse explained. She gave me a cold look and then left the room.

At that moment, I realized what I had done. I was not fighting a rival guy in the neighborhood. I nearly killed my own female closest cousin, Bree. She had been rushed to the hospital, but was released hours later. She was badly beat up. She was trying to help me when the snakes attacked me on the playground. As it turned out, the snakes were only the sand from the playground I had landed in. And when I thought I had jumped over a wall, it was really just the balcony from Bree's second story apartment.

I felt terrible about this and wondered, *"What's going on with me? How can I walk away from me?"*

I sometimes did not even know what was real or not. I snapped in and out of things. Life became a huge blur. No one could ever explain what happened to me or where I had been. It was like entering a vortex. There were many different stories, but the truth was elusive. And whenever I came to, there was nothing left to remind me of what really happened. I just had to pick up the pieces of my so-called life.

Now as I looked back, my life was a series of lost and sometimes gathered moments...

Chapter TWO

BLACK CAT & THE MURDERS

FAMILY. What can I say about them, besides that I was only in their lives for a short period of time? Things were not what they seemed to be in my family. With seven brothers, one sister, mother and stepdad, there were too many different personalities under one roof. There was always something not going right with all of us. As a family, we dealt with a variety of things, such as fighting, arguing, lying, and snitching on one another.

I always thought my mom, Tina, was beautiful on the outside, compared to other moms. However, I noticed that everyone seemed to be intimated in her presence. Grown-ups and kids alike were all scared of her. Most of my friends told me that she was a really strict and mean person.

Standing at about 5'5" and about 150 lbs., my mom was big-boned, with ultra-light blonde, shoulder-length, wavy hair. She had bright, hazel eyes. Tina always wore heels to make herself seem taller that she really was. Perhaps the height gave her extra confidence. Many of me and my siblings' friends would not come around, because if they did, they would be thrown out faster than if they even set one foot inside our house. She was constantly yelling or screaming at someone, including me. It was not a pleasant place to be.

For whatever reason, I could not get anything right in my mom's eyes. I got slapped, pinched, yelled at, or hit with any object within close proximity. Or just her hand. But the cruelty did not stop there. My mother was an evil woman. It felt like she made time just to think of punishments for me. I was her primary target of hate. Although I called her mom, it was without the loving feeling meant by the word. I mostly called her Mrs. Tina. She ended up having seven children all together; six boys and only one girl.

In contrast, my stepfather, Jacob, was totally different than my mother. He was a heavyset, Hispanic man with salt and pepper colored, short, straight hair and a matching beard, which he kept trimmed. He had dark eyes.

Most of the time, Jacob stayed dressed in his work clothes. He was a mechanic and seemed always dirty, with oil stains covering his body and clothes. His demeanor was laid back to the max. You could ask him anything, but he would usually say, *"Ask your mom,"* or, *"Yeah, why not?"*

Jacob never disciplined us or yelled at any of the kids. Although he was not my real Dad, he was the father to my youngest three brothers. He spent the most time with them whenever he had some down time from work. Whether it was playing sports outside or playing with toys inside, he was a dedicated father. Jacob worked a lot, so we did not see him that often. That is why he never seemed too upset, since he missed most of the big arguments and troublemaking that kids do.

My eldest brother, Joey was about seven years older than me. He was very popular at school and with the ladies. He was always the tallest of all the kids. He had a standard "boy look" with a medium build, light skin tone, dark brown eyes, and spiky short hair. Growing up, Joey was our mom's favorite child. He was always left in charge of all the kids whenever our parents were gone. He would often brag that we had to listen to him, although Joey was not that mean when he was in charge. He mostly did his own thing around the house.

In school, Joey was one of the brightest students in his grade. He got straight A's in every class, while still managing to play sports and maintain his high GPA. When he tried out for and made varsity football in his junior year of high school, our family was not surprised. We all knew Joey could make it; he was driven.

In his spare time, Joey could be found drawing scenery,

animals, people, or anything he thought of. Some were an exact replica of what he had been looking at.

Gabriel was the second oldest brother. He was the nicest one of all; very caring of all humans and animals. He liked bringing animals home that he found hurt. Gabriel nursed them back to health. Some of his animal patients made it, but others died. For those he could not save, Gabriel would do a burial ceremony and say a prayer for them. I attended some of these burials, along with my other brothers. They were usually very sad, but quickly done.

Gabriel had dark brown eyes, dark-to-medium skin tone, and was thin, with muscle mass. We were the same height. In school he was an average student. He barely exceeded the minimum to pass his classes. He was a loner and did not talk too much to people, including the family. He stayed away from home a lot, perhaps to escape the yelling. Boxing after school was his passion. Gabriel was a fast boxer with ability to throw quick punches in and out of the boxing ring. My family thought he was going to become a pro boxer, but he quit and dropped out of high school in the eleventh grade, at 17 years old. He never looked back at school or his dream to become the undefeated boxer. In later years, he shaved his head and preferred a bald look.

Number three was my big sister, Janet. I looked up to her the most. We would sit up for hours at night, whenever I snuck into her room to talk. She knew that mom was hurting me, but Janet felt helpless to do anything about it.

With beautiful, long, curly, dark black hair and eyes, Janet was a girly girl. She had a pretty mole on her cheek, light skin tone, and heathy weight in comparison with her 5'11" height. Despite her Hispanic bloodline, everyone thought she was Japanese. She always stood out whenever we went somewhere as a family. For me, those occasions only occurred when "Mrs. Tina" let me out of the house to go with my rest of my siblings.

Janet was also very pretty and popular in school. All the kids at school liked her and want to be friends with her. The boys followed my sister around like lost little puppies without a leash. Janet was very bubbly and interesting to hang around with.

I was the fourth child, and although my friends and family all called me Kris, my birth name was Michael. I never liked Michael. That is why so few people ever knew my real first name.

My skills were different than my siblings. I was always very street smart, I must admit. I knew the ropes and was often called a hustler. I did whatever it took to get that money to survive. Things were always unpredictable in the world we live in. It took me longer to get to know people. I would only let a few friends in at a time; to see what their true intentions were. I wanted to see if they were just pretending to be a friend, or if they wanted a free ride, or if they were willing to become a special part of my puzzled life. Like my siblings, I was always popular growing up. I was in soccer and loved wrestling. I was a walking dictionary; always reading to discover why things appeared the way they do. I've always enjoyed digging for answers to the inexplicable. As a child – and even now – I could be found thinking and daydreaming most of the time. At home, I spent my time staying out of my mom's way and doing my best to avoid her.

Robert was the fifth child. He was the second tallest and had the darkest complexion out of all the siblings. He kept his head shaved, with just dark, black, long, wavy, front bangs that he combed to the side. His eyes were medium brown.

Robert was always a bit heavyset. In school, he always got in trouble and skipped classes. His grades were low, but he didn't care. Instead, he chased the girls on campus. "You're girl crazy, man," I'd say.

Later on, I found out that Robert was experimenting and using different drugs with the bad friends he hung out with. Since we shared a room, I was the closet with Robert out of all my brothers. At the same time, he lived a totally separate life when he was at school. He'd disappear.

At school, Robert did not talk to me at all. Whenever I asked him why, he'd tell me it was for my own good. I knew Robert had a similar gift like me in seeing spirits. However, he was afraid of the gift and did not believe it was there to help him. He did not want people to be scared or hate him, like they did me. Robert's honest opinion of me really hurt my feelings.

The sixth child was Titis. Honestly, none of us knew if that was his real name, but that was the name everyone called him.

When I was able, I played with him; mostly when mom was not around to see me having fun. Titis was a couple of inches shorter than me, with a lanky body, light brown eyes, short, black, buzzed haircut and a ponytail on the lower back of his head. His head seemed way bigger than his body, which everyone noticed.

In school, Titis was a good student, great listener and made B's and C's. He never failed in his classes. He had a funny speech impediment, so he worked with his teachers to improve it, although it never fully came to fruition. He also played soccer with me. But Titis's favorite pastime was to ride his bike all over the neighborhood by himself, whenever he was home from school or on the weekends.

The baby of the family – and the one least liked by the other siblings – was Richard. He was the brat baby. He cried about everything. No matter what happened or who did it, Richard usually told our mother it was me.

Richard was very chubby; always stuffing his face with every kind of food in sight. He was also the shortest child. Like many of us, he also had short, black hair and dark brown eyes. He was always doing art projects in pre-school that would be displayed on our refrigerator. He loved playing with toy cars and taking anything else he wanted to play with. If Richard didn't get his way or whatever he wanted, he would cry until he got it. He was also a huge snitch and tattletale. The rest of us kids could not get away with anything, because Richard would run and tell mom the first chance he got. It was what he lived for. Each time, "Mrs. Tina" rewarded him with sugary goodness. He was her little, fat informant.

When I was a little boy – as much I can remember – my family lived in a two story, old, partially remodeled home. It was built in 1946 and had a total of four bedrooms. Two bedrooms were upstairs and two were downstairs. My mom's was downstairs. The room I shared with Robert was next to hers.

Being a light sleeper, I often woke up in the middle of the night. Sometimes I sleepwalked around the house. One night, I stumbled right into my sister Janet's bedroom! She never kept any curtains on the solo window of her room. I think I may have been four years old at the time; at least smart enough to know what was what.

Strangely, I noticed a black cat resting on the ledge of my sister's big window. The cat was watching my sister sleep. I sat by my sister's bed, watching the cat. This became a regular thing. I would wake up in the morning before everyone else, to see if the cat was still at my sister's window. But the cat was always gone.

I never saw the black cat roaming around the neighborhood. Sometimes I rode my bike around, looking for the cat, but I never found it. But every night, just like clockwork, that black cat was always right there at my sister's window; just staring at her. My sister once told me she was able to get the cat inside her room from the window ledge. It was a male cat. The cat was happy and purring while she patted him and watched TV. She started calling him Blake. He was so attached to Janet that he never left my sister's side, every night.

As I later learned, the symbolic meaning of cats is associated with guardianship or protection of home and people. Some neighbors, family and friends have said that cats are also loyal and master secret keepers. They serve as gatekeepers to the realm of other existence we are not a part of yet; the realm we call the afterlife. They say that black cats double in mystery and protective powers greater than mankind's knowledge. They are even powerful enough to keep negative energy away that might be directed towards you or your family. Some say they are good luck to have around your family and home.

Superstitious people claimed that black cats were used for evil-doing – such as omens and witchcraft – were things that people, to this day, still practiced. Satanic followers and cults used the black cat as strength to make deals with the devil. Superstition of bad luck was foreshadowed; if a black cat crossed your path.

My family and I were told stories that were passed on throughout many generations. We were supposed to make a cross over our bodies to protect us from any evil associated with cats. My family believed that if a cat crossed you, it was a symbol of death or horrible misfortune coming your way; possibly even your close, loved ones. Other stories blamed cats for babies that stopped breathing. The story was about cats getting on top of a baby's face, with intent to harm him. The superstitious people on T.V featured stories of cats who took every last ounce of their human's souls.

To me, the black cat was fascinating. I watched a T.V. program called, *'Cults in America'.* The show recalled Satan singing a beloved song. The narrators claimed it was the song to sing before you sent a cat as an offering to Satan. The black cat was sacrificed by chopping its head off. Afterwards, the cat's blood was poured all over the cult members' bodies. They tasted a sample of its blood, too.

When I heard the song, I liked it, but for some reason, I could not get it out of my head for weeks thereafter. It went like this:

Hush little baby, don't you cry. Kitty cat is going to take away that cry. Take every breath of air until you're dead. Suck it all out. Do not cry, it is your time; you are the little devil inside. That is pure and simple minded for the greatest of mankind. The greatest of mankind we are. For you, the leaders take this offering of ours to make us smarter and stronger to follow you to anywhere you wish. Child, last breath and black cat must die, to help their blood cleanse our soul to become your disciples of death. When darkness falls, die. You must submit a small sacrifice. So, hush little one. No more cries, little baby and black cat. Your time was traded up for the port to the power of mine, under our true king. Hush little baby, don't you cry. We took away that cry...

Have you ever stared at a black cat's eyes, so big and bright yellow? If you ever stopped to look closely, you could see yourself looking back at you through their huge, canary eyes. It is up to you to see for yourself and discover why this mystical creature is highly feared for its powers. Through myths and fairytales, I have heard of at least one incident in which a black cat was captured and burned to death on wooden stakes; mainly due to folklore and myths. Whether you think a black cat is good, bad luck, a beautiful pet or just a simple mindless animal, these are just some of the beliefs out there.

To me, the black cat represented a time when my sister was going through some rough things. The cat was trying to protect her as long as it could. That cat never looked at me; it just stayed focused on my sister. I am not sure if the cat felt or knew of my presence in the room. It probably knew that I was not a threat to my sister.

The black cats were among, before and soon after us...

My grandmother, Mary, was a short, Hispanic woman of about 4'9" high. She was a little chubby, with multi-colored eyes due to having cataracts. Her fair skin had a few wrinkles, with yellow, brittle, thin hair to match. She got it recolored every other month to cover up the white hairs that crept in more quickly with age. She was a spunky woman of 82, with a sailor's cussing mouth. Every other word she spoke was a bad word. You would never believe that she was a very religious woman.

Even Mary's home, where she lived solo, was filled with catholic statues of Jesus and other saints. She faithfully attended church every Sunday morning, never missing a service, even if she was sick. Being elderly, she was sick more often than an average person, although Mary was still of sound mind.

"Those doctors and medical people will end up killing me one day," Mary told me on many occasions. "They don't know all they think they do. I've stayed alive this far without them so I don't intend on using them now."

Grandmother Mary made me laugh all the time, especially when talking about family members or people that she crossed in her life. She never got married, but had three children. Tina, Gina, and Robert. My mom, Tina, was the oldest. Mary and I never really talked about any of them, except my mom. Gina and Robert both lived far away, in another state, and did not visit or keep in touch. Hence, there was not much to talk about concerning them.

But grandmother had stories to tell for days. Each visit with her was awesome. I adored Mary. She was world famous, in my eyes. From a singer, to a crossing guard; she had so many roles while raising her children. She did not really like the way my mother acted, but nevertheless, Mary came to check on all of us and make my mom's life as miserable as possible.

For example, grandmother would tell Tina she was a cruel mother who did not treat her kids right. She complained about most anything Tina did. It gave me laughter inside when our grandmother spoke up for us, but my mother did not ever see me laugh.

One day, when Grandmother Mary was over for a visit, I decided to confide in her. She was someone in whom I trusted more than any other adult.

"Grandma Mary, I have to tell you something," I said, trying to gather the words.

"Go ahead, boy," she replied, putting on her listening ears.

"I had a dream that there were handprints of blood on the hallway wall. But, they had been painted over... to kind of cover them up."

Grandma Mary gasped. "No way! I do not believe this. That's just crazy..."

Just then, my mother came stomping over to me. She had also overheard what I told my grandmother. "How dare you say that to your grandmother!" screamed Tina. "You just want attention, don't you?"

I hung my head. "No." I muttered. But she did not care,

nor hear me.

"Now stop embarrassing me! You will not say such lies, do you understand?" my mother hissed, right after she slapped me across the face.

Immediately, I retreated to my room in tears. I sat on my bed and huddled my knees against my chest. The crying would not stop, it was uncontrollable. "They do not believe me," I whispered to myself. None of my siblings could be bothered or even know what had just transpired.

That very night, I woke up as usual. I crept down the stairs to scratch on the hallway wall. Something made me. Something told me to go... to go scratch on the wall. The wall was between my room and my mom's room. First, I started scratching away one area and took a step back to see my discovery. It was of a hand print. Whose was it and why was it covered up with paint? I got scared and ran back to my room.

The next morning, I showed my mother. My mother scratched off the rest of the paint in that area and for sure; there were three hand prints of what looked like blood. After she finished scratching it all off, she turned and looked straight at me with a puzzled expression. It was a look of disgust, like something was wrong with me.

I could tell she was about to explode. "Get the hell away from here and go to your room to sleep! You'd best never talk about this ever again, you freak!"

The next day, the wall was painted another color. It did not really match, but I knew that Tina was the one who painted it. She had left some paintbrushes and paint buckets near the walls. She made sure to cover those handprints right back up, probably to avoid anyone else seeing what I had just showed her.

Meanwhile, my birthday was right around the corner. I would be turning six years old.

Growing up, we had a neighbor that lived behind our house. He always gave us candy, chocolate and all kinds of sweets. He was always so nice to us. We knew he lived all alone. My older brothers, Joey and Gabriel, nicknamed him '*Charlie Brown*' like the cartoon. I had no idea why, but back then, I believed that was his actual name. He was about 38 years old; 5'11" with a very thin build and always wore a very similar type of striped shirt. He had brown eyes, no facial hair, and dirty, short, blonde, wavy hair. He often talked to us and played games outside. Nothing creepy or weird. He was just a lonely guy trying to make friends with the neighbor kids.

Charlie Brown worked as a banker at a local bank. It was strange; he never married and lived alone in a really nice, huge, four bedroom house, which he kept very clean. Perhaps he was just a lonely man that no one ever visited.

He was very goofy and friendly, but my mother hated him. She told us to stay away from that other block behind our house and especially from that man. I never saw anything wrong with him. My two older brothers still talked to Charlie Brown, despite her warnings. I hung out with them, too. The neighbor had lived in his house for over eight years. He never acted inappropriately with any of us, but my mother was distrusting of him.

Not long after my sixth birthday, I started seeing different spirit images and having visons – sometimes even while I was awake. They were not just in my dreams anymore. I stopped telling my mother about the things I was seeing. I knew she didn't believe me and that I would get into trouble for telling her, too. Maybe she was scared of me because I was able to see things that others could not.

My mom was going through depression. Her relationship with my stepdad became violent. They argued about their problems just about every night. Things were getting pretty horrible on the home front. I would see her crying while cleaning or making food. Sometimes she would just sit anywhere in the house and zone out. She always looked depressed and never wanted me around her. In her eyes, I was bad luck.

"You are to never, ever open your mouths about anything you see or hear between Jacob and me, do I make myself clear?" My mom told us all one day. We nodded in compliance, knowing it was more than just being mad at each other. They were physically fighting at times, throwing and breaking things. We would all go straight to our rooms and I would cover my ears so I could not hear it all.

As much as I can remember, my mom had started abusing me by this time. She said the cruelest things to me and always made sure the others were out of hearing range when she did. She kept me right by her side at all times, while I was home.

I became a loner at school and highly introverted. My teachers started observing my lack of sleep and that I was very thin. They never saw the bruises or marks left behind from my mom's beatings. Sometimes it was even hard for me to sit down or stay in the same position. The belts, phone cords, her sandals, random tennis shoes, or anything else Tina got her hands on would become her weapon of choice. It was so painful, but I pretended I was alright. The abuse was a closed secret to anyone. Although I hid them well, the scars and bruises did not lie. I'm not sure why she singled me out. It was like a personal vendetta.

I became an antisocial child. Teachers, staff, my grandmother, people, and even other kids sometimes inquired about my deep introversion, but I denied it all the time. They knew something was wrong, but could not figure out what was causing it. The risk of my mother finding out that I had told someone was terrifying; so much that it prevented me from opening my mouth.

My attendance and grades were always good. One day, my teacher decided to call my mother to have a parent - teacher conference with her. My teacher wanted to talk about my behaviors at school. Before even meeting with the teacher, my mother grew angry. She waited for me to get off the bus and started screaming at me the minute I came through the door. "What are you telling the teachers??" she fumed.

"I did not tell them anything." I replied. I loved my mom, but I did not understand why she didn't love me back. I didn't understand what I did to make her hate me so much.

The abuse progressed to the point where my mother would lock me in her room after school, with no food or water. I stayed in there until bedtime and had to use the bathroom attached to her room and drink the water from the sink. Days and months went by. She never came to check on me at all.

One day, I decided to play with the water in the sink. Upon hearing laughter, Tina raced into the room and caught me drinking out of the sink. Things got worse for me then. She got mad and grabbed me by the arm to remove me out of the room. I thought she was going to rip my arm off as she dragged me out of her room and then upstairs. I was kicking and screaming in pain, but I was no match for the beast in Mrs. Tina. When we got to the top, she took hold of both of my arms and shook me extremely hard. Then, in pure evil, she said, "Oh no, my sweet baby..." and let go of my arms, as I was thrown down the stairs.

It was like slow motion. I remember my body flying in the air and then rolling down the stairs. My head, body, hands, and legs all hit the stairs and railing at different times. When I landed at the bottom, there was blood coming out of my mouth. I couldn't move. I just laid there, ready to die. She was still screaming at me. "Now go to your room!" she bellowed, but I guess she didn't realize how badly I was injured. I did not even have the strength to get up when she ordered me to.

Then, Tina disappeared for a bit. I overheard one of my siblings asking if I was going to die and or if I was okay. My stepfather, Jacob, had been asleep when she went to him to ask for help. He ran up to me with tears in his eyes.

"Pick him up and put him in the car," my mother ordered. "I guess I'll have to take him to the freaking hospital since he hurt himself."

As Jacob lifted me up and put me in the car, he whispered in my ear, "I am truly sorry, little man."

Mrs. Tina drove me straight to the hospital. The ride there was pure silence. I figured she was trying to conceive a story to get out of the situation. Plain and simple, my mother nearly killed me. As I faded in and out of coherence, all I heard was the car shifting gears in a rough, hurtful, bumpy, ride to the ER.

When we got to the hospital, Mrs. Tina drove the car right up to the hospital doors. She jumped out of the car, leaving me still inside with the engine running. She started screaming dramatically, "Please, help us! My baby boy got hurt. He was in an accident. He fell down the stairs. Dear Jesus Christ... please watch over my child." Tina was melodramatic, as if she truly cared.

Within minutes, I was rushed into the hospital and sent to my own, private room. Doctors and nurses hovered over me, doing various things to mend the damage. I remember them giving me some medicine and I must have been put to sleep. When I woke up, I overheard Tina telling the doctors and nurses that I was horse playing with my brothers and fell down the stairs. They never once asked me what happened. Mrs. Tina pretended to be worried about me whenever the staff was around.

I stayed only one night in the hospital. After taking lots of x-rays, it was determined that I did not break any bones. Luckily, I was just badly bruised. However, I know this incident scared Mrs. Tina by her actions.

After I was discharged from the hospital, Mrs. Tina let the staff help me back into the car. She kept thanking everyone for taking such wonderful care of her baby. I just rolled my eyes. I still felt drowsy.

The ride home was not quiet. This time, she sang really loud with the music from the radio. I think she was proud of her actions and herself. She had done it again. Mrs. Tina, my mother dearest, got away with abusing me yet again. I could see her looking at me through the rearview mirror; just smiling, while she sang along to her songs. When we finally returned home, she parked the car and went inside. As I sat there, buckled to the backseat, I just waited several minutes before my stepfather came out to get me. Jacob unbuckled me and lifted my badly bruised body. I was still in a lot of pain. He silently carried me as tears just kept coming out of my eyes and falling from my face. I could not keep them bottled inside anymore. The struggle to remain alive was real – while living under Mrs. Tina's roof – under her hatred, watchful eyes.

"Dear God, this has to STOP," I prayed silently.

Several weeks passed by. After the hospital incident, Mrs. Tina stopped keeping me locked in her room. I wondered if that horrifying 'accident' might have prevented her from hurting me again. *"How long is this peace going to last with my mother?"* I thought to myself.

I was seven years old when I started starving myself. My only thought was about survival. I was not hungry during the day. The thought about food or even wanting to eat was nonexistent. My appetite was gone. I would only eat in the late afternoon when I saw my brothers and sister eating dinner. When I was allowed to, I sometimes ate with them. I was scared of my mother I didn't know what to do anymore. Simple things, like saying that I was hungry, needing help with my homework or asking to please go to the restroom became scary.

I had no one to talk about my friends – the dead people – those whom I could see or talk to when I was alone; away from everyone. I tried to tell my grandmother Mary again because she was the only one who seemed to believe me and my visions. Unfortunately, she stopped me from talking about it and told my mom right away. As a punishment, Mrs. Tina told my stepdad to rig her restroom sink so that no water would come out anymore and all that was left was the toilet to use in her restroom. So once more, I was trapped in her bedroom again. This time, there was no running water from the sink to drink. After a couple of days, I was so thirsty that I decided to drink out of the toilet bowl. I had no choice. It smelled terrible and was so gross, but I got so dehydrated; there was no other option for me.

Perhaps my mom felt that by keeping me away from everyone else, things would be normal and settle down. I think she blamed me for her relationship with my stepdad when they got into real loud, bad fights. I did hear my name involved in between their arguments. Jacob referred to me as, "*your animal*". After hearing him say it several times, it saddened me. I just wanted to be loved like the other kids.

I wanted someone to understand what I was going through with these sightings. I didn't want to harm or hurt anyone. I was not lying either, but no one believed me. I often wondered, *"Why doesn't anyone in my family ever stand up to Tina? Why don't my other siblings ever get into trouble like me? For no reason?"*

My mother hated the sight of me. She always looked at me with a face of disgust. She would tell me that I made her sick and she wished I was not her kid. Sometimes she would spit at me. She would grab me and jerk me around sometimes. She would leave marks and scratches on me. I went to school like that, covering it up as much as possible. I felt like an outcast; that is why I kept away from everyone at school. I maintained a low profile and rarely interacted with anyone while I was there. I did not want anyone to tell my mom that they suspected what she was doing to me. I was so terrified of what she would to me if the school called her once again to talk to her about me.

My stepdad Jacob would sometimes bring me a banana and other fruits to eat. He would tell me where to hide the peels or cores of the fruits. "Whatever you do, please do not ever tell your mom that I gave these to you," he'd say. "If you get caught with them, just say you brought it home from school. Better yet, hide it."

In their master bathroom there was a lower bottom cabinet that held the toilet plunger and other stuff we did not use. There was a small hole directly in the wall, with a piece of board covering it. It was approximately 5" x 7" around. Jacob showed this hiding spot to me. "Leave the peels and what you do not eat there," he instructed. "I will throw it away at another time for you."

"Thank you," I said gratefully. I did not understand why he was helping me, but I was so happy to see him come in with that fruit. It was the best feeling to enjoy biting into those fruits and get a little sustenance for my empty stomach. Just a moment of satisfaction went a long way. Especially since Mrs. Tina would not let me eat for the whole weekend or after school, until it was time to go back to sleep at night.

Months went by and I started getting lonely, so I would put myself in her closet with the lights off and talk to myself. It was complete darkness. I was so lonely and miserable being locked up in her room. I would ask GOD, *"Why does my mom treat me this way? Why doesn't she love me? How can I make her love me? How can I change the way I am? Am I going to die? When is this going to end?"*

I would cry myself to sleep right there, in Mrs. Tina's closet.

By the time I turned eight years old, I knew I was not going to have a birthday party, but I still looked for any gifts from my grandmother, Mary. She made sure not to forget to celebrate my birthday, especially since at my house; it was just another day passing by.

Nevertheless, Mary brought a piece of cake and a gift for me. "You are special, Kris. Don't ever forget that."

I believed her, even though I did not feel or think I was so special. "Thank you," I said, unwrapping the birthday present. Inside was a toy doll named Woody, from one of my favorite movies, *Toy Story*. Woody was the well-liked, loyal, friendly, smart, sheriff for his community in the cartoon movie. He had a thin body, light skin tone, reddish-brown short hair, and light brown eyes. He wore blue jeans and a yellow, long-sleeved shirt with black stripes. Around his waist was a belt with a cowboy belt buckle. He wore dark brown boots, a brown western hat, and white and black cow-print vest with his Sherriff badge on the left pocket. Everyone loved Woody.

This was the kind of person I wanted to be when I grew up. I always kept my toy Woody doll with me everywhere I went.

All I wanted was for someone to love me and to become my dearest friend. I was so lonely and depressed all the time. I never smiled or laughed. I went into the dark closet at least every other day to cry and talk to myself.

One day as this was happening, a voice coming from the back of my head responded. In a calming, low, voice I heard someone talking back to me. "Don't be afraid anymore," he said. "I am your friend sent to guide you to freedom on the other side. We can escape together from this horrible life you have been living. You will be free and never will be hurt ever again."

I was not scared at all. The voice spirit did not frighten me for one second. I was actually relieved to finally have a friend to share my feelings with. A force who would respond back to me in a conversation of some sort is what I badly needed. The spirit had no name to me. I never gave him a name. Instead, I just called him "friend".

My friend was a new spirit. I assumed he was from the dead – trapped here on earth with us – the living. He seemed very interested, intrigued, concerned, and wanted to help me. I could not see this spirit, unlike others in the past. I could only hear his soothing, friendly voice near my ears or around me. I was able to tell which direction the voice was coming from each time. We would talk for hours about school and what I would love to do the next time I got out of being locked in my mom's room. He would say he was going to save me and grant me wishes. I would not have to cry anymore and I would be free at last. I just had to wait for it to happen.

"All of life's wonders are now at your disposal," he'd say. "Just be patient. All in due time. You just have to wait... *wait for the time to be right.*"

"I hope so," I countered. I believed it. I believed my life was going to change and that things would get better for me real soon. He brought me joy. He was a true friend that cared about me.

After several nights, the spirit that I had been talking to appeared to me in a dream. He had taken on the shape of the Woody toy doll, perhaps because I was so fond of it. He told me his name was "MOMO" and he had transformed his soul into my toy doll, Woody.

"Keep me with you at all times for protection from the cruel world!" he said. "The toy doll shall not leave your side."

Now I knew his name. My only one true friend. Momo, Momo, Momo; what a friend! I woke up saying that to myself three times. I finally knew my friend's name. I was so happy that I got out of bed and ran to my toy box to get my Woody toy doll. I picked him up and said, "Your new name is Momo, not Woody anymore." I hugged him tightly and went to get ready for school that day.

Meanwhile, my brother Robert was still asleep in his bed and did not wake up with my excitement. I did not know much of what possibly evil things Momo had to do to get transformed into my doll or why he was sent to me. I did not even care about any of that. I was just ecstatic that I had a new best friend that was here for only me.

That same year, I discovered that our friendly neighbor, Charlie Brown, had passed away. I never found out what really happened to him that caused his death. He did not smoke and was against people doing drugs. *"Oh no,"* I thought to myself, *"No more free chocolates anymore."* It was his time to go to another life.

Charlie Brown had been one of the few people I could talk about seeing ghosts, spirits and visions. Prior to his death, he had told me a story about the house that we were living in. He asked if I could handle knowing that information.

"Yes," I said. I was curious about it, at any rate.

Then, Charlie began talking in a slow, low, voice. "Years before your family moved in, that house stayed empty. No one wanted to buy or rent it, until you all came along and moved in. But since you all have been living there for years now, I think you should know what happened."

"Go on…" I said.

He went on to explain. *"The last family to live at that house was a family of five people. The Dad was named Sam. He worked at a metal factory that made car parts. He was a white guy in his late forties, a little overweight, and about 5'9" tall. He was a bald man. Sam's wife's name was Terry and she had straight, strawberry blonde hair with green eyes. She was a stay-at-home mom, of average weight and height. They had three children, ages nine, eight and three; all boys. The nine-year-old was Logan; he was the eldest of the three. He seemed to be the quietest one out of the bunch of boys. Always looked serious and would get after his other brothers to follow instructions.*

Then there was Eric, the eight year old. He was a blue-eyed kid with short, wavy, dark blonde hair. Eric was a cheerful, fun loving, and laughing kind of young boy. He was the one that seemed not to follow instructions the most.

Last, there was little, adorable, three-year-old Ayden. He was green-eyed, short and had wavy light blonde hair. He was a scrawny kid but very friendly, loving, smiling, caring, and an adventurous little child.

There was always abuse going on and cops being called every other month to that house. From what I observed, the father, Sam, was a raging alcoholic who often stayed out late. By mid-morning of the next day, when returned home, a fight would usually start between the husband and wife. It escalated really quickly. The whole neighborhood could hear them, including me. The three boys were seldom seen playing outside; just going in the house or leaving it for school. They were adorable little boys, but very disciplined. You could definitely tell by the way they followed each other in an orderly manner.

Sometimes when the mother Terry would be seen walking around outside of her house, the neighbors and I would try to talk to her. We knew she was a battered woman. She kept her head staring down towards the ground and whenever we did see her face, she seemed distraught. We all wanted to help her in any way possible. But Terry would always stop and look our way and then put her head further down and quickly walk back inside. She always looked like she had been crying. Her clothes were three times too big for her, which was probably from losing weight and not eating much in such a depressed stage of her life.

One day we heard arguing and loud breaking of glass and things. Almost twenty minutes later, we heard five different gun shots. By this time, I was on hold talking to the cops when I heard the gunshots. Some were right after the last one and some were minutes in between. Then it all got quiet; a total stop of silence in the night. Within five minutes later, I heard one final gun shot. I started screaming at the operator to hurry; this was not good at all! Meanwhile, I paced back and forth, trying to look out the windows facing your house.

The cops showed up minutes later. Within an hour, there was caution tape all around the house to keep everyone a distance away. Soon we all saw the media, ambulances, lots of extra police cars and homicide units arriving to investigate. Then, we saw bodies in black bags being wheeled out of the house, one-by-one. A total of five were brought out.

The media reported it was a very sad and horrible execution and suicide by the battered mother. The media never released the children's names, but the parents' names were mentioned several times on the T.V. and in newspapers. The husband Sam was found hunched over his bed, shot twice. Once in the right back shoulder and one on the side of his head. The nine-year-old boy, Logan, was shot in back of his head. His body was found still lying on his bed. They claimed that the middle child, Eric, tried running out of the room that he shared with his older brother Logan. He was shot once in the heart. The news crew stated that that Eric left bloody hand prints all around in his room near the door and throughout the hallway leaving his room. This is where his frail, little, bloody body collapsed, right in front of the stairs, just feet away from his bedroom. They were assuming that the eight-year-old was the only one to face and see his mother Terry shoot him.

The baby, three-year-old Ayden, was shot in the chest while in his toddler crib, where they found him. The mother Terry was the one on the shooting spree and finally she shot herself through the head with one shot.

It was a horrific story that was told for many years' over and over. No one would go near that house. Everyone knew it was possessed by the family, especially the children's spirits that remained trapped in the house. Until... like I said, your family moved in. We all wondered what would happen to you all. The coroner at scene stated that the mother, Terry, died instantly. The other family members did, too. The exception – he determined – was that the oldest son, Logan, stayed alive for over thirty minutes, while bleeding to death. No one in that family awoke after going to sleep that night. No one survived that dark, deadly, evil, night. Their poor souls stayed trapped in that house, never to leave alive again."

Chapter Three

3:36 A.M. & Evil Plays

Late one night when I was about nine years old, I overheard my mom telling my other brothers, Joey and Gabriel, to turn off the T.V. "This is a school night," she said, sounding annoyed. "It is too late and you need to go to sleep for school." They complied.

Hours later, I snuck upstairs when I heard my mother yell at them again. "I thought I told you guys to turn off the TV!" she bellowed from her room.

I peeked in my brothers' room and they were both still asleep. The T.V. was on, but there was no show on. Just an empty channel making a loud, lost, signal noise. I heard her scream louder, "Hey, you better turn off that T.V!"

I did not want to get caught being in their room, so I turned the T.V. for them and rushed back down the stairs to my room. After a while, I heard the T.V. turn on again, so I got up to see who had turned it back on in my brother's room.

Gabriel and Joey were still asleep, so I quietly turned it off again. As I was tiptoeing out of the room, the T.V. turned on yet again, but this time, it was really loud. I turned around in the direction of the T.V. This time; it had woken up both brothers. They thought I was playing with the T.V.

Just as I started to tell them I came in to turn it off, they said, "Get out! Go back to sleep and stop playing around with the T.V. or we will go wake up mom."

Now I was getting scared, so I went to my sister Janet's room and asked to sleep in her bed. I told her that I was hearing noises. She agreed to let me sleep in her bed. I still couldn't go back to sleep, so I sat up on her bed all night long, hoping the T.V. wouldn't turn on again.

At 3:36 a.m., I looked over at my sister's alarm clock. I heard someone running up and down the stairs. I thought it might be my two little brothers, Titis and Richard, playing around. I got up to check. But as I peeked out of my sister's room, I saw little leprechauns. There were three of them. Something was definitely not right about them. They appeared to be blurry, but I could tell they were all short and hairy guys. All of them had bright, yellow eyes.

One of the leprechauns reached out for my hand and another grabbed my other hand. They started running up and down the stairs with me. I started laughing loudly because it was so much fun. I did not realize how loud the noise of running up and down the stairs was. It woke up my mother. She came to the stairwell and asked, "What are you doing up so late? And why are you not in your room sleeping?"

"I am playing with my friends. Look, do you not see them?"

"See what?" She looked confused.

I pointed at the leprechauns. They just stared at me, standing still, not moving, kind of frozen in their spots. I started to describe them to her, "They're short, with yellow eyes..."

My mom interrupted, clearly agitated. "There is nothing there, go to your room."

As I started walking down the remainder of the stairs, the leprechauns disappeared. I could not see them anymore. I did not understand why my mom could not see them too. I was not scared at all and instead wondered if – or when – the next experience would be. I hoped that I would get another chance to see and play with them again. But I never saw them after that brief moment of enjoyment on that mysterious night.

The next day, I tried to tell my grandmother Mary and my brothers Gabriel, Robert, Titis, and Richard that I had seen these leprechauns. But before I could get into the story, my mom overheard me and interrupted. "Shut the hell up! You were sleep walking and dreamt about them."

I looked at my mother and spoke defiantly under my breath, "You're lying. I was completely awake, you know I was. I even tried to tell you what they looked like and everything."

Upon hearing this, Mrs. Tina threw a frying pan at my direction. I shifted enough that it barely missed my head. The pan hit and knocked down the living room lamp, which shattered into pieces. I ran to my room. "That's right..." my mother screamed after me, "You'd better get out of my sight right now!"

So I did. I hid in my room under the bed. I did not know if she was going to come after me or not. I trembled under my bed, crying... waiting for the beating to happen. I fell asleep under the bed, where I remained until the next day for school.

I found the incident with the leprechauns fascinating enough, so I wanted to learn more. The next day at school, I went to the library to find some books that might give me some clues. What I learned was that the appearance of the leprechauns in threes was highly powerful.

The leprechaun is a magical, fairy folk creature created by God's realm. Leprechauns always appear to be males, never female. They typically have a mythic, short stature with long, bearded, facial hair. Just look for that pot of gold at the end of a rainbow. Some say, "Do not let those cute little green fitted men fool you."

If you look back in time, the first signs of Leprechauns were shown wearing red, with dark, creepy, bright, yellow eyes. By befriending you, this may lead you to believe they are the work of good. However, Leprechauns are disguised as pure HELL. They are only after your souls. Usually they come out when summoned by an evil force. Only a few have been able to get away and live to tell their story. You might even think the devil was behind these evil beings.

Upon reading this, I slapped the book shut. I wondered if the devil was trying to take over my young soul. Actions might suspect the devil had already begun trying to do just that...

As time went on, my mom abused me every time she had an opportunity to do so. Both mentally and physically. Sometimes she would strike my fragile body with her bare hands, but most of the time, she threw objects at me. She attacked me mentally by telling me that I was worthless, a little whimpering faggot, useless, retarded, and a freak of nature. She constantly said she was disgusted that she created me from part of her very own flesh.

One time, my mother told me I was a *"waste of sperm and she wished she had gotten an abortion, if only she would have known how I would come out."*

That hurt me deep in the core of my heart. I responded right back to her and blurted out, "Momma, I am made out of your flesh and blood." She turned right around and slapped me on my face so hard I fell straight back to the ground. I was left there crying. It cut me so emotionally deep to hear those words come out of my own mother.

Another time, she said, "I must have gotten punished for doing something in the past by having you as my son." On and on it went. I was a loser and shit was better than me. Supposedly, I was the devil's bastard son. Whenever she said these horrible, hurtful things, I would just look away and continue crying. I allowed her. What could I do? I was a child and no one would believe me anyways?

Indeed, Mrs. Tina was so vicious at times. I could never expect the things that would come out of her venomous mouth. It was like getting poison injected in me, but instead, all the words absorbed into my memory bank, a place where there were only deposits and never any withdrawals. These hurtful, crushing things that were said to me on a daily basis crushed my soul and my spirit. I was broken and I knew I was not well because of my mother's cruelty for so many years.

Where was her heart? I often wondered. *"I am her son. Does she not realize that I still love her, despite all she has done and is still doing to me? Can this stop? Please God, make her stop,"* I prayed at times, begging for forgiveness for whatever I had done. My siblings witnessed so much, but everyone ran away and stayed out of her path. I cried myself to sleep so many nights.

During my teenage years, my mother had a business she ran out of the house. That was how she made her money. It was a small, office administration business that handled so many different things for a client. Her business did work from creating documents, preparing taxes or managing expenses as a financial advisor. I was like her secretary. I answered the office phone, took messages and set up her appointments in her day runner scheduler. I also handled the paperwork and got it organized in sections for her. Mrs. Tina gave me directions on what to do, but then stood right next to me, watching to see if I made a mistake. If I did and no client was around, I would get knocked on my head or hit on any part of my body.

It had to be done methodically to her specifications. Otherwise, it was unacceptable. I didn't really read the whole document; I just did a quick scan to see what it was and prepared it just the way she instructed. It had to be in a particular order each time, or I would get beat up in some way from Mrs. Tina. I had to learn everything quickly and perfectly, without any mistakes.

Every project had different colored folders and sections to be put in order. A red folder meant that it was a harder project that would require additional hours of research and work to complete. A yellow folder was simple and those were usually given to me to process, since Mrs. Tina would say that even a monkey could comprehend these tasks. It was all a part of her so-called, 'ordered office procedures'. She worked on sections at a time. Some jobs were higher priority, so they went into a purple folder and had to be placed on a pile right next to her phone on her desk. A green folder indicated the project completion, which meant that it was ready for me to call the client to return for the finished assignment. I would charge each client before we started any process for them.

Every weeknight, I had to press iron her clothes and hang

them up in front of her closet for her to put on the next morning. To me, she dressed like she was a lawyer; very business attire for her small business company at the house. I made sure that Tina's coffee was made and ready for her every day before she got up.

Although I did not really have the education yet to do this job, my mom gave me onsite training. I managed to learn how to do things quickly and right by her rules. She taught me how things had to be done at her office. I always felt like my mom was jealous. She did so by bringing me down or waiting for me to fail. But I did not. I figured it all out, sometimes just to disprove her and other times to avoid the backlash of abuse that came with any mistakes.

During this time, I was also discovering my gifts of magic, tarot card readings, talking to spirits, souls, ghost, and animals. Some of the clients who came into the office at our home wanted to see me, to know the wisdom I carried. That crushed Mrs. Tina each time she heard them ask for me, instead of coming for her services. I could tell by the way she looked at me that she wanted me out of the picture and hated me. I never knew why some clients could believe and feel my powers.

My younger brother Robert was always close to me and would tell me all the mean things that our mother said about me when I was locked away in her room or had to stay in her office fixing things for her next day of work.

Throughout my childhood, I was in search for answers. I

would ask myself, *"Why can I see these things and others cannot?"* I was able to see the ghost and spirits walking around among us, in the house, all hours of the day. This occurred not just at home, but everywhere else, too. These spirits would look right at me and I would look back at them. Some were not happy about it, and those ones always got me scared. I knew they were real.

Not all of them could touch me, but some would tap me on the back or shoulder; just to give me the feeling that they were with me when I couldn't see them. *"Stay away! Leave me alone!"* I'd say to those spirits who scared me. I kept my distance from them, since I knew some could not leave and were trapped in a certain place.

I often had visions of Mrs. Tina doing tarot cards to learn more about me and my life. It was strange, because I lived in the same house with her, but she only did this when I was at school. I held a lot of feeling in the things that I have dreamt about my mom. Every time I had a dream of her, she was hurting me in so many ways.

I later learned that my conception was a mistake and my mother did not really want to have me. My father did not want me, either. He was upset that Tina was pregnant and told her to get rid of me. My birth father did not want anything to do with me or my older brother, who was not even his child. When she did not follow through with the abortion, he left. That was the last time she ever saw him, which explained a lot of the reason why she held so much resentment towards me.

After I was born, Tina met Jacob, my stepdad. She went on to have my younger siblings with him. Hence, I was the only child from a different man. This explained a lot of her hatred towards me, although it was inexcusable.

Mrs. Tina once hit me with her office metal document hand sorter. She hit me so hard on the top of my head. She was mad because I was playing in the walkway closet in the first floor of the house. It was such a hard hit that it gashed my head open and blood started gushing out. I remember seeing blood streaming from my head. I was crying and trembling in an emotional state of shock. I must have passed out with a concussion right after that.

When I woke up, the following day, I was in my room with a plastic bag under my head. There were white bandages covering the wound. Rather than offering any sympathy, my mother told me to follow her into the restroom. She cleaned and serviced the huge gash in my head with peroxide first and then packed it with instant coffee powder before bandaging it back up.

After I returned to my room, Mrs. Tina gathered all of my siblings together. I heard her telling them I was ill and was not able to go to school for a while. I did not go to school for about two weeks. She lied and told the school I had chicken pox. She kept me away from the other children '*so they would not get ill*' too. All of this was a cover up lie for busting my head. I never went to the hospital or saw a doctor about it. I did take the bandage off once to see it and it was about 3 inches long. Then, I wrapped it back up the best exact way it was done before, so that my mom would not notice.

Tina did not really have any gifts like I did. She wanted to, but I knew she was just doing what she read or heard about. I warned her not to try any "*love spells for dummies*", even if they came with step-by-step directions. She got scared when I told her this.

"Are you jinxing me?" she asked.

"No, I'm just warning you," I replied.

"If you had never said that, it would not ever happen that way," she said. My mom blamed me for everything. It was always my fault, even when I tried to protect her of doing harm back to herself from her very own black magic love spells.

"I'm telling you, do not do your love magic on Jacob because the spell will backfire on you. Like, he will go crazy or try to hurt you. I'm just letting you know," I added.

In many ways, I hated my mom for the cruel, painful things she did to me, but deep down, I couldn't stand by and let her hurt herself by performing various '*black magic spells*', no matter how small they seemed to me.

"How do you know?" she asked, ever the know-it-all.

"They do not work if you are not familiar with the spell. It will backfire and put bad magic or karma on whomever is doing the magic spell," I answered.

She did not know whether to believe me or not.

Chapter Four

MOMO & THE DEVIL'S DEAL

I can see energy and karma... and I can read people by sight. I was just ten years old when I recognized my gift, and knew it was getting stronger. I did not understand how to control it. Momo was my precious, adored friend inside this little doll. When the doll had been given to me as a gift for my eighth birthday from my beloved grandmother Mary, it was a special toy doll that I played with and took with me everywhere. Once it became possessed, Momo was a living dummy I used to play with. He lived and thrived through me, yet he was a voodoo doll of black magic that created despair to others. I came to realize there was more to him than meets the eye. Some qualities were not so nice to be around for others. Total control of Momo was never granted to me.

People could not mess with Momo. There was a price to pay, although repentance and groveling on your knees might save you for a while. I held the strings and felt that Momo was incredibly strong.

Momo was the first voice within me that I heard; while sitting alone in the darkness of my mother's closet as a child. That voice was Momo all along. With that first whisper, he let me know that I now had support to help me out of the misery I was dealing with. Momo used to live inside of my Woody doll before he came into me.

To me, Woody was a superhero. I could relate to his character in the movie '*Toy Story*'. I watched it all the time – over and over – replay after replay. It was my favorite movie. I pretended I was Woody by saying his lines with him. I wanted to be like Woody.

Momo made me do selfish things. He told me to stop thinking about everything and everyone else, and instead to think only about fun for me.

There was a huge difference between Woody and Momo. Woody always tried to help his fellow toy friends and others. Momo, on the other hand, caused pain and hurt to others. He was very manipulative and mentally violent. He enjoyed hurting people's feelings. He liked to create chaos in people's lives by making situations go differently or by changing the outcome. He antagonized people to his advantage by turning them against one another for his self-gain.

"Just let it go," Momo always told me. *"Do not care about*

anyone."

He seemed to feel nothing about anyone. He only cared about me. He got mad when I refused to do certain things. He'd punish me by making bad things happen or by losing a friend. He pushed and scared others away.

Momo was ageless. He seemed to know everything and be everywhere. I felt like he could never die and that nothing could stop him.

As I grew up, Momo was around a lot more than just the nightly visits in the closet. He was in my head, always telling me what to do next. Years went by and I knew he had taken over my life. Momo was one of my voices I heard, which I knew was somehow inside me. He would hurt so many friends past, current ones and those that crossed our path. Everyone would follow what I said it was Momo and never addressed directly me. Especially knowing Momo is me too. New people who came into my life would leave frightened by something Momo did. If they called me to beg for forgiveness or to apologize for something they had done to me, I would say, "You need to apologize to Momo, not me. He is the one in your dreams."

There was silence on the other end of the phone.

"What was it he did to you?" I would ask.

Some would tell me in detail. One of Momo's victims gave the following, bone-chilling account after being attacked in his sleep:

"I keep having night terrors – seeing horrible things happening to people I care for – or happening to me. When I woke up, I knew that Momo had something to do with it. I felt his presence and demonic vision appearing in my nightmares. Many times, I woke up praying for them to go away and to please leave me alone. I would tell him I needed to make things right with you and to ask for your forgiveness. Then, to never see or be part of your life again. I need to stay far away from you."

Another person's experience went like this:

"I experienced sleep terrors; episodes of screaming, intense fear and flailing, while still asleep. Falling asleep became a safety risk for me. That demon with yellow eyes called himself Momo. He grabbed my neck, and I felt the sensation that something was being rammed down my throat. I was being held down by a force stronger than multiple men."

I remember one guy whose entire body trembled as he spoke. He started crying to me. He pulled up one of his long sleeves and revealed his arm, carved with a letter "M" stamped over it. He said;

"This is Momo's mark he left on me. The curse followed me. I know it is him because I see the symbol of the beast left behind in my nightmare. Sometimes I can hear a voice when no one is around – calling out his creepy name – Momo. Pictures began falling from walls when I walked past them. The doors

would close by themselves. I experienced these freaky random accidents, when I know I didn't fall or hit myself... it's all him. I am so terrified of what else Momo will do to me. You and Momo... please, just leave me alone!"

This one girl wouldn't even look at me. She was too scared.

"I had to jump into my sister's bed because I was too scared to sleep alone. Bad luck and a string of misfortunes happening in row, that's no coincidence. I was one of the marked ones by Momo.

I woke up with cuts and bruises on my arms and legs. In my dream, I tried to escape, but Momo had cut off my legs at the knees to prevent me from leaving. In some of the dreams, I could only remember pieces of it. I would just wake up screaming and terrified. My stomach was in pain and blood was on my shirt. When I lifted it up, I found a carved mark with this one eye shape and a letter "M" over it. It was still dripping with blood. Sometimes I woke up from someone hitting me in my dream. My body could barely move. I have the marks of reminders – of whatever or whomever I pissed off – which were you.

It goes on... I dreamt about hanging out with family and friends. At the time, I didn't realize they were all dead and talking to me. It gave me chills, especially when they grabbed me or changed voices. I could hear scratching on metal and people calling out Momo's name. It was always dark and creepy in my dreams and this horrible object would show up with yellow eyes, intensely watching me.

I was in my room and no one else was home. I heard a lady laugh and a man calling out a name to kill myself. I came out and opened the door. No one was there. I checked all the rooms. I know I heard them. Then, once when I was driving during the day, my electric car seat started moving me up and down. The safety belt got extremely tight on me, right over my neck. It was too much for me! I had to stop and jump out of the car.

While I am driving, I sometimes get the feeling that someone is poking me. I feel eyes or see something sitting right in the back seat while I'm driving.

The other night, it got very cold and the air conditioning wasn't working... but my room was like a freezer. Then I looked at the dresser mirror and it had an eye symbol with an "M" on it. I know it is MOMO! I just know it is him. He wants me dead."

Another girl sobbed while telling me her story...

"I sprung out of bed because I couldn't breathe. I started waving my hands to make noise. Then, I started hitting my boyfriend to wake him up for help. He woke up and was freaked out. He had no clue as to what to do for me. He told me I was turning dark reddish-blue. He said that my eyes had changed to a bright yellow color. He finally laid me down and tried to give me mouth to mouth. In her nightmare, a dark shadowed person had put a rope around my neck and was dragging me across the living room. When I was able to breathe, we walked to get me some water. My boyfriend was holding me and calling a nurse

link at the same time. When we walked through the living room, it looked like there had been a real struggle that occurred like in my dream. I ran to the restroom to check out my neck. I had deep rope burns around my neck. There was an eye mark with an "M" over it. Momo attacked me that night."

My little brother Robert also had the gift of seeing the dead among us. He told me of an experience he had through one of his nightmares:

"In my nightmare, there was a doll that I found while walking down the street. When I picked up the doll, it talked to me and said its name was Kris. Then, I started to hear the name Momo and my name too, being called repetitively. The toy doll then transformed into a large, husky man who was trying to hurt me. I tried fighting him, but I was no match for whatever it was.

The evil being put a spell on me that made me blind. I woke up right away and my body was all sweaty. I couldn't see for a couple of minutes, but my sight eventually returned. I did scream for my other brothers and when they got into the room, they all saw a big, dark, black, shadowy circle moving away from me."

Momo had already warned and prepared me about my brothers all coming to help me. He told me exactly what to do. When they got ahold of me, I told them that Momo is really a doll, but he does not let you see him. He doesn't want you to know how he looks. He will hunt you like deadly prey. Each move was precise to get into your mind and make you feel trapped by great sadness. It made your skin crawl. Momo enjoyed it and laughed while telling me these stories. No one could run or hide from him. He was everywhere and caught you every time; to leave his mark on you.

Momo loved to haunt people in their dreams, making everything dark and frightening. If you incurred his wrath, you became his target. There was no escape. You became paralyzed to fight back or get out. There was constant shaking and mumbling words that came from the darkness, but the real fear struck by just being anywhere alone.

Momo especially haunted my mom. Of course, she never told me what kinds of things Momo did. But she was always chanting verses of prayers to help fight demons. She'd say, "I know. I can hear you call the name Momo while I sleep. Leave me alone! You're a sick boy."

It was all Momo. I could see it happening before it really did. Momo showed me through his visions. He used black magic to get the dark forces to line up and cause hell to them. He told me exactly what he was going to do to each of them. He would say, "They deserve pain and I am the person to give it to them. They will pay for hurting us. I want them all to know me, Momo. I see and am watching you. That is what my mark means. It is a symbol."

I was too afraid to stand up to him, because he would do the same thing to me while I slept, if I disobeyed him at all. I just had to say '*I wish this or that would happen*' to someone and look at a picture of them. Then, Momo made sure that my thoughts came true. He would use black magic. He used crystal rocks and black sand and he would do a reading from a book written in a different language, which learned was Islamic. He performed dark curses, hexes, and bindings to whomever stood or got in his way. He was very powerful and feared by all that met him, including me.

Satanic Witchcraft was his playground. Momo loved to create chaos to all. He gained strength in making people suffer in pain. Revenge spells were his specialty. When he met someone new – within seconds – he already knew if they were good or bad people. I felt him getting stronger with each year that went by.

I noticed that I was always chilly when Momo was around. A shadow followed me, as if it was a shade of my body. It was really Momo, watching and waiting to strike. In evil and complete darkness he lived. I began to wear dark sunglasses at night to hide my eyes and disguise my true identity.

You would not survive if you looked into my eyes. Momo could hound you with those eyes day and night. Even if you were awake or asleep, he was over you. His presence crept into your body, taking away the air and crushing your sense of security. You were his toy to play with however he wanted.

One night, I remember Momo asking me, "If I could grant you only one wish, what would it be?" I did not know what to say or think. I was a bit shocked because I knew he would want more from me. What else does he want from me? I was going through so much; my mother was still abusing me and keeping me locked away while I was at home. I felt caged and isolated from the world. I was depressed and wanted to end this pain. I felt alone. My only friend was Momo. I did not have any other friend, not even my brothers or sister. I wanted a better life away from all this misery. My family did not understand me or sympathize with what I was coping with in my life. I felt sad.

Despair is the feeling of not having any hope left. I started thinking about his question and told him, "I just want to be happy." That was all I could think of to reply.

That night, I went to sleep and was awoken by some dark force. I felt its presence right away. It made me shake and I almost peed in my pajamas. It was way more powerful than Momo. What or who was it? I got out of bed and looked toward the closet. I saw yellow eyes staring right at me. The coldness consumed my body. I heard the deep voice asking me, "You want to be happy? I will bring happiness to you, but you have to give me something in return. Is that a deal?"

I said "What do you want from me? Are you Momo?"

He laughed.

Then I asked, "What do you want?"

"I want just one simple thing, your SOUL!" The dark shadow stated.

I said, "No way. Forget it."

"Did I hear you deny me?"

My body then rose from the ground about three feet and was thrown. I could barely get up. I didn't know what to do. Trembling and crying for the spirit to leave me alone, I tried to think. Finally, for some dumb reason, I said, "I need time to think about it, but first, you must give me my happiness."

Later that night, Momo appeared with an evil grin. "You made a deal with the devil. You sold your soul! But don't worry, friend, I will talk to him for you. You will be happy, I promise that to you. Trust in me."

A few days went by, Momo got pushier with his request. "So, when are you going to give your soul to the devil? He wants you..."

"Please, just leave me alone."

A fresh new school year started. I was only thirteen years old and in the eighth grade. Something about the first day made everything seem like it was going to be a better experience than the last, especially since this was my final year of middle school.

On my first day of school, I walked to my homeroom class. My teacher was Mrs. Sanchez. She taught Spanish at the Middle school. Mrs. Sanchez's dark, black, short, curly hair bounced as she walked around the room. Her black eyes glimmered when she smiled. Looking at her, you might expect that she was a mean lady, but she was the sweetest, most well-liked, down-to-earth teacher I'd ever had.

Mrs. Sanchez was both my homeroom and Spanish teacher. Every time we listened or answered questions correctly, she rewarded us with candies and privileges, or by not having to do assignments or with extra free time to do other things. I adored her and was considered the teacher's pet. I did anything that she required assistance with, such as passing out papers, making copies, erasing the chalkboards, picking up papers, and updating the board with monthly topics and discussions we were having. I did not learn much Spanish in her class, but she still gave me a passing grade.

I started talking to this guy from school named Kevin. At 5'7", he was as tall as me, but he was fourteen; a year older. He had stayed back one grade in elementary school. We met in Mrs. Sanchez's homeroom class on the first day of school. He came in and sat in the desk adjacent to me. He stared at me for a couple of minutes. His full, 210 lb. size with all that short, wavy, black hair atop his pale skin with freckles made him look like a dirty Q-Tip. His deep, penetrating, eyes were framed by silver-rimmed glasses.

Finally, I asked him, "Are you a new student to this school?"

He responded, "No, I have been for the other two years. I've seen you before, but never talked to you."

I started to laugh. "Well, if you never talk to me how, are you supposed to know if I am cool or not?"

He said, "You are so right."

The class started and he wrote down his phone number and passed it to me with a smiley face next to his name on a piece of paper. After class, Kevin walked out first and stopped me right in the classroom door. He said, "What is your schedule? Let us see if we share any other classes?"

I got out my itinerary. "Oh yeah! Besides the same homeroom class, we share two classes; English and Phys-Ed."

Kevin handed me back my class schedule. I smiled and replied, "I look forward to seeing you in our next class, so please save a seat for me, buddy." I started to walk away, but decided to look back to see if he was still standing there and looking at me. To my surprise, he was. He smiled and waved at me. I did the same and turned right back around to run to my next class. It was good to have a friend.

The day passed so quickly; by the time I knew it, English class was here. When Kevin saw me, he hollered, "Over here, Michael! Sit here."

I moved towards the seat and we started talking about how the first day was going and other random things. He did the same thing for our last class together. I swore, it seemed like Kevin was rushing to each class to make sure I got a seat right next to him. He seemed like a sweetheart and nice person to talk to.

Kevin liked me, but I wanted out of this city. We started spending more and more time together at school and afterwards before I had to go home. I always pretended to be in some afterschool project, so my mother would not know. My friend Kevin worked in the school office, so he fabricated 'pretend' school function letters for me to give my folks. After a while, I asked him to help me to run away from El Paso, Texas.

He said, "Yes, I will. Let's go to San Antonio. I have people I know there. They will help us out."

Then it dawned on me. I realized my wish was coming true; a new happy life. *'Oh shit!'* That meant the Devil came through and now I owed him my soul for sure. What was I going to do?

That night in my room, Momo came to me very upset. "It is time to give up your soul, Michael."

I screamed back at him, "I am not going to give the devil anything! I do not need it. Tell him to take it all back. He can take whatever he wants from me, but I decided not to give up my soul to the devil. I am not sacrificing my soul for anything."

Momo was in rage. I did not see or hear from him for almost a week. I knew I was going to get it, but what was my punishment going to be? Then, Momo started haunting me too.

I saw the devil a couple of times. I saw him in my dreams. He was just a stranger. Once he was a blonde lady with short hair. She was sitting on a bench and wasn't looking at me. She just kept talking to me, asking me what I was I doing. She wanted to know so much about me and who mattered most to me. She seemed so caring. I did not realize I was giving out so much information. We were just talking naturally. I had no clue what she was up to at all. Then when she turned around and looked at me, it was the devil's face grinning.

The second time was in another dream. I was having passionate sex with this random guy I did not know. I was really getting into it and then the light from the window shined on his face. Oh no! It turned into some random old wrinkled man. I stopped right away and tried to get out of the bed. He was just smiling at me. Why would he do that and keep smiling too?

When I realized it was an old man I was having sex with, the human turned into the devil. "Get away from me!" I just backed up to the bed to try to attack him, but my brother then disappeared. I felt disgusted and ashamed of what I had just done.

The third time, my sister Janet was showing me a recording that I had on my phone. I asked her what she was doing, as I sat in the living room. I asked her to see the recording and I tried to turn to see it better. Something grabbed my hand. It threw me far across the room. I feared it was the devil.

The fourth time, I killed Momo in my dreams. I was choking the breath out of him. Then he turned into my brother. But I kept going, knowing it was a distraction. It really was still Momo I was choking. After Momo died in my dreams, he turned into the Devil.

I kept having visions that my mom sacrificed me. My mom performed love spells on her husband to make him stay with her. She would put his name in burning candles. She would add his picture with writing of what she wanted from Jacob on the back of the photograph, while it continued burning. When caught my mom doing these things, something always told me that she was really evil. I always wondered why I got these visions about her doing things to me, wishing I was dead.

Chapter Five

MICHAEL THE ARCHANGEL

I Michael was a wonderful, sweet, gentle, guy who was very good in ventures or anything he touched. He was a very truthful and friendly person. He loved everyone and had no ill feeling toward anyone he encountered. He was a huge motivator to all. He made things happen. He had an uncanny way of knowing exactly what needed to happen for the best outcome.

His favorite snack was hot Cheetos. He was a normal, American guy. He was a hard-worker on his after school jobs, smart young man who made his money the right, clean, way. He was very respectful and did not cuss. Michael was '*that perfect guy*' everyone wanted to be in a relationship with. He personified what my life should have been like.

My mom wanted me to be like Michael, but I could not

live up to those expectations. I tried... but I could not be him all the time. Michael was the guy I wanted to be, but the voices in my head would not allow it! After a while, being unable to live up to being as good as Michael tore me up inside. I told people, “Michael is dead. Stop calling me by that name. I don’t like it. That is not my name.”

Although my first name was Michael, I always hated that name because I knew it came from my mother. She loved that name. I wanted to be called another name *Israeli.*

Michael wanted the normal life growing up. He did not want to be gay. He felt like gay people came into this world to be somebody in life – to be like those celebrities in the spotlight – not to live the simple life of a married man going to work. Michael believed that by being gay, he had a true, inner demon. He thought gay people were loners because they were never satisfied with who they had in a relationship. He surmised that some guys liked both boys and girls because they were undecided about what they really wanted.

My mom always told me that the name Michael came from the bible. Michael was one of GOD’s angels. That is why she gave me that name; to be like one of GOD’s angels. Michael the Archangel was a very important individual in heaven. The name Michael had an important meaning: "(one) *who is like God*". Archangel means "*chief of the angels*". Yet Michael the Archangel, in contending with the devil, when disputing about the body of Moses, dared not bring against him a reviling accusation. He said, "*The Lord rebukes you*!" Jude 1:9

When I was Michael, all I wanted was to be loved by everyone. I thought he was a great guy, trying to find his true love. He searched high and low to find her – the love of his life – wherever she was. The one that was the rib to his existence; like Adam and beautiful Eve. Michael wanted to live in the future world even though he was still a child he dreamed of being an older married man with children. He wanted to enjoy a fulfilled relationship with a wife, together as one, supporting each other in parenting their children as a team.

This dream included that proverbial white picket fence with dogs running around in a great, large yard. He dreamt of 'ever after' love, like in the movies. He wanted simply to find the one person that seemed to complete him – who knew how to help in any situation – sharing stories, secrets, insecurities, decisions, and laughter. Sometimes Michael felt so lost without his soulmate.

Michael was the spiritual one. He was a healer and removed peoples' curses. That was one of his main gifts. He even healed people that were unaware of what he was doing. They never knew what he did for them. He did not tell them, because he felt as though they would be scared of him for doing it.

When my mom took me to doctors and different hospitals to find out what was exactly wrong with me, I was never told if anything was diagnosed. When I got home from an appointment, my grandmother would explain that I had a powerful gift from God.

"Habilidad y etras un don mijo," she said in Spanish. It meant, *"You are and have a gift of leadership qualities, gifted speaker, and have a way with people, son."*

I would whisper when I talked, with a low voice. I never wanted my mom to hear what I was saying, so I whispered. I did not want to be noticed by others, so I hid in the shadows of every room. If I was out of sight, I was out of harm's way; from the abuse of my mother.

The strangest thing about my childhood was there were not any pictures of me. From infant to teenage years, the only pictures I saw were from my grandmother in Mexico. We had taken a group picture when I was around nine years old. I never knew what I looked like as a baby, or growing up.

I never met my real dad. I did not know what he looked like. My grandmother Mary described him to me once. Her description was not very nice and I could tell she did not like him one bit. According to her memory, my father was about 5'11" tall, ugly, dark complexed and of Indian heritage.

Grandmother Mary told me that my mom had met him at a College football game when their rival school played against one another. She said he lived in a two-story house. She was in a committed relationship to him but he didn't feel the same way towards her. As the babies kept coming he never was around for the births or any occasions. I would tell your mom to stop seeing that low life boy. As you know she didn't listen to me back then nor does she now. When my mom told him about being pregnant with you her fourth child, he didn't believe for some odd reason you were his. Soon afterwards he moved out of his apartment and simply disappeared. He was never seen again. My grandmother never mentioned my real father after that tale.

Perhaps this was one reason why my mother made it perfectly clear that she did not like me and felt like I was her personal failure.

I was very close with my older, only sister Janet. My sister and I had a bond. I knew her secret when she ran away. I was the reason she ran away from home. One weekend afternoon, I was outside helping Janet put the laundry on the clothes line. I studied her for a minute and stopped hanging the clothes. I looked straight into her face and said, "You are a couple of months pregnant. You are going to be showing very soon. I saw a vison of mom cutting off most of your hair to make you look like a boy. She also made you have an accident. I do not want to tell you what happened to you."

Janet stopped hanging clothes and started crying. "How do you know these things? How is it possible Michael? You need to tell me my fate when she finds out."

I did not want to tell her. I begged her not to make me say it. "All you need to know is that the only answer for you and your unborn baby is to run," I told her. "Run far away from mom and do not look back, for your baby's sake."

Janet grabbed me and shook me forcefully. Tears rolled down my cheeks. I said, "Please, sis... you are hurting me. Please let me go! Fine, I will tell you."

Crying, I began telling my sister the awful vision...

"After I saw mom cutting your hair and slapping your face – while calling you nasty and mean things – you got up to run out of your room and go downstairs. Mom pushed you and you fell down the staircase. Like she did to me when I was little. You were pretty hurt and in pain from your stomach area. I saw blood forming all around your body, while you lay lifelessly at the bottom of the stairs. Your baby died."

Janet started screaming, "This is not real!" Then, she ran to her room.

The next day, my sister came to me and apologized for hurting me and asked for my help. I told her not to worry. I would find a way for her to leave without anyone knowing she was gone. I had to think about it. That night, I went to my sister while she was asleep and told her, "Mom is knocked out and stepdad is still at work. Now is the chance for you to leave while you still can."

"Won't mom hear me and wake up? What if she finds out?" asked Janet, a little worried.

I told her, "No she is out cold. I just checked on her again. I made her coffee and put some sleeping pills in the drink. I stole the pills from the drugstore earlier today. Now, leave sister and be careful out there. I love you."

She hugged me. "I will come back for you when I get settled," said Janet. "Give me a few months... maybe even a year."

I followed her to the front door and closed it, but did

not lock it. Then I went back inside to go to sleep.

The next morning, mom woke up screaming for my sister. "Have any of you seen Janet?" she asked in a panic. I shook my head no and lied back down on my bed. She finally realized that my sister had run away. Mrs. Tina and my stepdad went driving around looking for her, but they did not call the cops about it.

Janet had made it out of this hell. My turn was coming; I knew it.

That same year while I was still just thirteen years old, we suffered another loss in our family. One of my younger brothers, Titis, died. He was only seven. It was a thundering, rainy day in El Paso. El Paso had so many mountains, all around the city. There was a ditch that came down from the mountains. We were all outside playing in the rain.

My oldest brother, Joey, was asleep in the house. He was the one mom left in charge to take care of all of us. The winds were strong, pushing us around. I shouted to my brothers, "C'mon guys, it is raining a lot! We should all go inside." The nearby ditch was filling up fast with water.

"No!" replied Gabriel. "Let's make boats before mom comes back home, instead." So we all started playing, making things float in the ditch.

My gut told me to go inside. I looked up and saw a vision

of someone floating in the dark, gray clouds. I left my other brothers at the ditch and had to jump back over the wall next to the ditch to get back to our house. After about twenty minutes, everyone returned back to the house because it was starting to be really bad outside. The rains were like a monsoon.

All of my brothers came back. "Where is Titus?" I asked. He was six years younger than me.

"He didn't come," said Joey.

Richard went to tell my oldest brother that Titis did not come back. In a panic, Joey went to look for him. "You guys stay inside and wait for mom or me to come back."

Not long thereafter, we heard firetrucks, ambulances, and police all around our house. Titis had somehow fallen into the ditch and got swept away with the rushing water. Some of the firemen tried jumping in to rescue the little boy's body, but it was too late. Titis drowned in the ditch near our house.

It was the saddest day of my life. I prayed and asked God to forgive me every day. I realized that I did not love my family the way I was supposed to, but I knew I was God's child. There was a reason he made me go through all these hurtful events; to become a stronger person. I believed that Jesus loved me, too.

Chapter Six

ISRAELI & A DARK SÉANCE

I was fourteen years old when my mom convinced me to go see her tarot card reader. I did not want to go, but Mrs. Tina forced me by threatening to hurt me again. So, I had no choice. Survival mode was my life story at this juncture, so I followed her commands. Thinking about the past years of beatings and abuse at the hands of the woman who was supposed to love me weighed heavily on my mind. I did not know how much more I could take.

It was a dark, windy night when she decided to visit her. Mrs. Tina had been going to the same tarot card reader for several years. She always asked her the same question involving me. The lady would not give her the information or answer the questions my mom asked.

"What powers does my son Michael have? And is he gay or straight?" she imposed upon the tarot card reader.

"I cannot answer this," the woman would reply, each and every time.

"Well, do you know if he would ever harm me or anyone else in the family?" Tina asked.

"The only way to get the information is to bring him here one day," said the woman.

It took a long time to drag me there, but the threat of more abuse was a strategy that worked well for Mrs. Tina. When all else failed, she knew how to push the right buttons. My mother also knew that I had a gift of reading tarot cards too, and held suspicion about having someone else read my cards. She had stumbled upon me doing the cards for myself one time.

On another occasion, I tried doing a reading for her. But my mom freaked out and never wanted me to read her cards again.

The tarot card reader's business took place at her home. The rickety old place sat on a corner lot in a rural part of town. It was a big, old, wood structure that looked as though it would fall to pieces any day. Walking up the front steps of the porch, the wooden boards made creaking noises with every step we took. The tan, brown paint had cracks all over the siding.

My mom knocked on the door. Cob webs hung all around the door frame. An eerie, low, raspy, voice said; "Come in." When she spoke, the woman sounded elderly.

We walked into the house. Mrs. Tina went in first and walked at a normal speed in front of me. I followed slowly behind her. The smell of animal feces permeated as we entered the horrible house. I trudged slowly through a long, dark, hallway filled with pictures of relatives and activities hanging up. There were different saints and other collectibles that cluttered the walls, which were symbolic of a hoarder.

A cold breeze brushed my skin as I squinted my eyes to adjust to the dimness. A light shone from a distant room as my mom and I walked towards the voice. When we got to the last room, I stood in the doorway, frozen. A strange, wrinkled, and oddly-dressed old woman sat waiting for us in a high back chair. It was decorated eccentrically, such as her clothes. Her deep, dark, huge, black eyes had heavy bags under them. They looked straight into the darkness falling all around me. The tarot card woman's hair hung straight and long; with loose strands that floated eerily around her head. The white of her hair glowed under the dim lighting.

There was a round table in front of her. Right away, I saw the deck of tarot cards stacked neatly, just to the left of her hands. A big, crystal ball sat on an iron claw in the center of the table. There were colored, small crystal rocks all around that ball. I smelled incense burning. However, the darkness made it impossible to see.

Religious fixtures were hung and displayed all around the room. They hung on the walls, and some were clipped to the dusty curtains. Figurines hid in corners, or on shelves, peeking out to stare at her visitors. I could feel their eyes boring into my skin.

The tarot card lady told me to sit on the chair facing her, across the table. I did exactly what she requested. I knew the lady was a witch and that she was not trying to help me at all. She was looking into my eyes. My eyes roved around the room to avoid staring at hers. I sensed this was not a good visit for me; however, I was not going to help her get into my head or see into my mind. She wanted to help my mom hurt me, and I knew it in my gut.

Before she began, she looked at my mom. "Would you please go wait outside of the house?" she asked, but it was more of an order. "And don't come back inside until I'm finished."

Without hesitation, my mother simply replied, "No problem, I will be right outside waiting."

My mom never looked at me or my direction. Instead, she exited quietly. I could not believe she left me alone with this woman. She must have really wanted this lady to get deeply into my head. As for me, I was very nervous and somewhat scared of the whole situation I was left to deal with on my own. Not really knowing what this old hag wanted to find out, I just hoped this reading would be over with quickly and that I would not get hurt in some way.

Without my mother present, the elderly, creepy lady started talking to me. She was breathing heavily and kind of whispering words to me. I could not make out what she was saying or asking. She would be talking and then stop to gasp some air and then continue talking. It was as if she was trying to do a séance.

I had heard about these things before. A séance was an event in which the living sought to get in touch with members of the spirit world and beyond. It typically happened when a group of open-minded people gathered to create a welcoming atmosphere. Then, they tried to invite spirits to answer questions or deliver messages from those who had passed away. Holding hands or closing the eyes helped to bring in the spirits. Candlelight helped the deceased to make their way to you when calling for them. The one main rule for conducting a séance was that everyone present should believe that it is possible to communicate with the other side.

Although communicating with spirits was frightening to most people – because people tended to fear what they could not fully understand – the vast majority left the experience with a sense of wonder and appreciation for the world beyond what they knew to be real.

In the midst of her ritual, the tarot reader witch pulled out a plastic bucket from under the table we were sitting at. Inside the white plastic bucket, she grabbed ahold of a bloody animal part or organ and held it. She chanted the same sentence three times. It was in another language. She sacrificed the animal. She needed it to perform the black magic on me. I could not tell what it was when the poor animal had been alive. However, the terrible, lingering smell almost made me vomit.

In her raspy old voice, the woman witch instructed me, "Stand up now."

On trembling knees, I did what she told me to. I did not want to end up like that poor animal in the bucket.

"Take off your shirt and pants." Her voice sounded like nails in a can. Her finger looked like a skeleton as she pointed and spoke. "I need you to cover yourself with that red towel over there in the corner of the room."

My body was trembling and my heart was beating rapidly. I thought I would pass out with fear. I saw flies circling around the white, plastic bucket. She started pouring the blood all over my body and chanting a group of words repeatedly and quickly. Then, she picked up a sage smudge stick and said, "I am giving you a sage shower. Listen closely to the directions boy; I need you to cup your hands over the smoke and 'wash' your face with it, then wave it all over your body as you would when in a water shower. In your mind, visualize any residual negativity fleeing out of your body and into a space of oblivion."

Something in me started laughing loudly. I could not stop the laugher.

The elderly lady suddenly stopped the séance. She tried to look straight into my soul. "You do not have an evil angel," she said. "You have two angels by your side; guardian angels. There is going to be success in your life. There will be two important guys who will become part of your life. One will be called '*Moreno*' in Spanish. His first and last name both start with the letter D. He will have a very thin build, dark short hair, brown eyes, about 5'8" in height and will be a very nurturing young man. The other one you will meet in the future. He will be what I call a '*Wero*'. He, too, will be a very successful person; 5'11" tall, 175 lbs., short, wavy, black hair, and brown eyes. He will be thought of as a humanitarian type of individual. He will explain and share your story. He will know all your secrets and the things you do not want to tell anybody."

I stared at the tarot card reader, listening with intent. She kept talking. "You will also meet a young white lady with short blonde hair that is around your age. I cannot see too much of her."

I knew that the name Moreno was a Spanish nickname for someone with dark hair and a swarthy complexion. Wero was a word used in Mexico and some parts of Central and South America to denote a person of fair complexion.

"Now, wash yourself with the other towel next to the bucket of fresh water and put your clothes back on." Still shaking, I quickly wiped the blood off my body wherever I could, but I wasn't doing such a good job, especially on my back. As I kept wiping, she said, "I need you to sit back down, so we can continue on this spiritual realm to uncover the truth of your being here on earth among the living."

As she spoke, I kept wiping off the blood. '*What is she*

going to put me through next?' I wondered. I cleaned as much of the blood off and as I put my clothes back on, I felt like I did it really fast. Then, I returned to my seat in front of her again like before the blood bath ritual.

She sat back down; giving the tarot cards a strange look. "Your force keeps blocking me," she said. "Why do you continue resisting and blocking my visions and cards? What are you hiding? What do you not want me to see, little one? Let me in... I can help your powers."

All of a sudden, the lights turned completely off and the cards moved on their own. Either an evil or good spirit force was present in the room with us. The witch lady looked at me, fearfully. "Why did you move the cards? Did you move them with your mind?" she asked in a scared, shuddering voice.

I was terrified by the whole ordeal already and wanted out quickly. I had nothing to do with the lights turning off or some of the cards being flipped facing up in a circle.

The tarot card reader jumped up, looked straight at me and screamed, "Get out of here now, evil let me be! I order you to leave now!"

Right away, I got up and ran out of her house. My mom was sitting in our car where it was parked in the driveway. I ran up to it and got right in. "We have to go now," I told her.

Mrs. Tina was not happy. "What happened? What did you do?" She got out of the car to go back in to the card reader's house.

She realized it was locked. She kept knocking, but the

door did not open. Finally, Mrs. Tina gave up and came back to the car. She looked at me and said, "I know you did something to her. I will find out, believe me. I will find out what you did."

My mom seemed very upset and kept driving, without saying any other words or looking at me on the drive home. I was so glad it was over and I knew I would not see that crazy lady anymore after today. I was rid of her. Now, I had to wait and see what kind of punishment I got for this situation. I already surmised that my mom would inflict some kind of pain to me.

A full month later, I walked outside near the open kitchen window. I heard my mom talking to my stepfather Jacob. I stood there to eavesdrop on their conversation. She had returned to visit her tarot card reader, because the woman was not answering any of her phone calls. Mrs. Tina said when she arrived, the home had caution tape all over it. The house had been abandoned. "The room must have caught on fire and burned to the ground," Tina explained to Jacob. "You know, it was the room that she read the cards to Michael that day we went to visit."

Suddenly, the window was shut by my mom. I could not hear anymore after that.

Although most of the visit with the woman had been very strange, I was enlightened to know I had two guardian angels. The one with the top of his wing broken was named Israeli. He was the angel I would always ask for help anytime I was in danger or needed help. He saved me from all my problems.

This was my spirit guide, for sure. He was a God of Protection. The ancient Egyptians saw him as an Earth God. When I realized he really was Israeli, I got excited.

Israeli was the one that got me out of trouble and kept me out of jail. He was my protector that took me out of harm's way.

For instance, about a week after I had visited the tarot card reader, I was ordered by Momo in the middle of night at 3:36 a.m. to get out of bed. His instructions were very clear. "Go to the kitchen under the sink cabinet," he directed me. "There's a pair of plastic gloves. And look up on the counter for a lighter. Then, go outside to garage to get the gas can for the lawn mower. It still has gasoline in it. Grab your bike and get on and start riding."

I rode my bike for hours; I was exhausted. Finally, I was standing in front of that tarot card teller lady's house. I was wearing the plastic gloves. I wanted nothing to do with this, but I had no choice; I had to complete the mission I was assigned to do. It was just a week after being there and this time it was payback for Momo.

I left my bike on the ground at the front of the house. I proceeded straight to the back of her house, just outside the room where she did the awful stuff to me. I began to throw the gasoline all over the wall outside of the house. I still had the gloves on as I got the lighter out of my pocket and looked around for a scrap of paper to light it with. I found a small, paper wrapper on the ground, picked it up, and walked over to the wall of the house with the fresh gasoline all over it. I lit a piece of the paper on fire and then threw it at the wall. Within seconds, the fire grabbed on to the house. Before running back to my bike, I watched as the flames started to crawl up the wall. I grabbed the gasoline bucket and fled.

I rode my bike so fast; I forgot how far I had just traveled. I was almost back home when I took off the gloves and threw them onto the cold street. As soon as I got home, I put the gasoline bucket back where I had found it in the garage, threw my bike in the backyard and went inside to go to sleep. I was extremely overwhelmed with what had just happened. I got in my bed and started crying, asking Israeli for help to get me out of this situation.

Then, I fell asleep. When I woke up, it was like nothing happened. As the days and weeks went by, I watched the evening news or read the newspaper whenever I got the chance; to see if anything was ever mentioned about the card reader's house being burned down. I never saw or read anything. That is how I knew Israeli was saving me from getting punished and going to jail. Too bad he was unsuccessful in his ability to prevent Mrs. Tina from hurting me anymore.

The way I summoned Israeli was through tears. When I start crying, he came to me. My pain was his pathway to save me. He came to me with open wings to carry me away from my agony and pain. He wiped away my tears with a brush of his wings. His comforting acts of companionship and love always made me feel safe. In his presence, I was at peace; a bit sheltered from all the hate and negativity coming at me.

There were a few things I learned about Israeli. He was born in B.C. era. He used a lot of nature's cures for healing. With him guiding me, I learned to make remedies for optimal healing. He taught me to use natural ingredients like leaves, eggs, limes, tea, and cactus, which I rubbed all over my body whenever I needed healing. His voice was tranquil, putting me at ease and comfort. He helped me to drop the walls and barriers so that I could be myself without any insecurities and judgements.

I feel that this relay of information is streams of my consciousness blurs of heavens gold knowledge. The passage of time presents from the past to the future. Be a light unto yourself and others. There's nothing more beautiful than inner peace. Salvation is in one's life. Live now not past or present. Love is blind even when looking through it with your own eyes. Love yourself. A visualized image begins to be experienced in their formless nature. Sacredness comes from the heart of within me. I greet the heart of sacredness within you.

It was he, my Guardian Angel Michael, who taught me about the spiritual gifts. Streams of thoughts were replaced in my mind, that which I was thinking. "We do not see God in others because it is in our mind," he told me, silently. "We fail to see God in ourselves, so we cannot see it in others. The knowing that one can be free of death is power itself."

Chapter Seven

LOVE ME OR LEAVE ME

By the tender age of fifteen, I had adapted to living in survival mode, because that was all I knew. I did not know how else to function, since that was my entire existence. I often found myself asking, *"If I asked my brothers or sister for help, what would they do?"*

I loved my mom, Mrs. Tina, but at the same time, I did not want people to know. I started talking to my grandmother Mary more and finally told her what my mom was doing to me. She was outraged. My grandmother never knew the whole ordeal of mental and physical abuse that Mrs. Tina was doing. I always thought my grandma knew and was too scared to stand up to my mom, but as I started talking and showing her the scars that I had hidden, she was dumbfounded. With each scar, she listened to the stories of how each one occurred. Her reaction worsened, as she listened.

Grandmother Mary had not realized who was actually harming me. When I told her, she started crying and promised to protect me from even her own flesh and blood. She decided to take me away from living with my mom and told me that she would become my guardian and take care of me. I was so excited! I could not believe I was finally leaving the house of hell I had been living in, under the care of the monster that was supposed to be nurturing. Instead, my mother inflicted vicious, hateful, acts towards me.

While still living with my grandmother, the living situation was a great deal better. My grandmother took wonderful care of me. I always had hot, nutritious meals ready for me. I was allowed to sit with her at the dining room table. I had my own room and even privacy to enjoy it on my own. She signed me up for therapy to begin the process of healing from all of the pain I had endured over my lifetime.

Even with better living at my grandmother's house, I felt I had suffered enough in the city where I grew up. Plus, I had seen my mom off and on throughout the months. I remained in the same school, but my siblings for some reason refused to talk to me. They kept their distance away from me while at school. I never talked to Mrs. Tina; just my siblings over the phone for a few brief minutes. But things were different. It was like I was not part of the family anymore.

Whatever she told my brothers kept them away from me. I was done with trying to be loved by her or being a part of that family. Obviously, I didn't belong with them. I could not allow her to hurt me anymore.

I was still in a relationship with Kevin. It was hard since we were living such a distance away from one another, after moving in with my grandmother. We talked at school, but mostly kept in touch over the phone or by letters we gave each other during school.

When I was sixteen years old, Kevin and I finally decided to leave El Paso. School was out for the summer break, so we decided to go to San Antonio.

We had an older, guy friend named Peter. He had told us he was 32, but we both suspected that he was lying about his age. My guess was that Peter was in his late forties. He was a bald headed man with brown eyes, dark brown skin and about 230 lbs.; 5'10" or so. He was our school janitor the last year we attended.

Peter had befriended us one day after school, on the football field. After we got to know him, he always talked about eating and playing video games at his apartment. He was a nice, friendly, and helpful guy to us. Usually he had some snacks and treats for us to share after school. I did not have any bad thoughts about him; I just figured he must have been a lonely guy without any friends. He often invited us to his apartment – but I lived so far away – and Kevin would not go to his place without me.

At any rate, when Peter overheard us having a conversation about leaving the city for good – and going to San Antonio, Texas – he interrupted. "Hey, I know people in San Antonio," he said.

"Oh yeah?" We both chimed.

"You know, I've wanted a change of scenery, too. I was already planning on going there after the last day of school. I already started the hunt for a new job and apartment there."

The wheels started spinning. "You would take us with you?" Kevin asked, already reading my mind. It did not take much convincing.

"Sure, I'd love to take you guys. It would be nice to know you there," said Peter. "Just leave a letter to your families to let them know you are leaving to start a life together as a couple and that you do not want to be bothered anymore. Tell them you want to just live your lives in peace."

Kevin and I wrote similar letters to our families. Mine was just to my grandmother Mary, whom I would miss very much. I thanked her for the great care she had given me, when no one else in the world had. Peter told us to pack up whatever we had that would fit in a bag we could carry. Our plan was to meet in front of the school on the first Friday of summer break, at exactly 11:00 p.m.

The plan worked out great. My grandma and Kevin's family were all asleep. We spoke on the phone right before we both left our houses. With just one huge duffle bag, I snuck out to move to the next phase of my life. Kevin was on his way too; with just a backpack and another mesh bag filled with his belongings. We were doing it to be together. We both had only $50 dollars to our names.

At precisely 11:00 p.m., I got to the school and Kevin was already there, waiting with Peter. They talked about the new life we were all going to be having. We piled into Peter's car and drove to our new destination; San Antonio, Texas.

The ride was a long; over eight hours. Peter stopped the car twice for food, fuel and bathroom breaks. Besides, we all needed to stretch our legs and get out of his crappy vehicle. Kevin and I only gave Peter $20 for gas at the first stop and told him we were sorry that we could not help much more. It was nothing compared to what he had to pay. We figured we'd use him to get where we wanted to go. So, Kevin and I took turns messing and flirting with him. We did anything to make him feel good, so that Peter would not regret taking us with him.

Once we arrived in San Antonio, Kevin and I did not know where we were going to live. Peter had mentioned while we were driving that he had already rented himself a small apartment in a duplex house. Apparently, Peter said we could just live with him at his apartment for as long as we wanted or until we found jobs and could get our own place. Plus, Kevin told him he could play with us while we were there with him, since we could not pay for anything until we found jobs.

All three of us were going to live in a one bedroom apartment together. Less than three weeks went by before I got a job at a local restaurant nearby. It was called Sonic Burger Stop. Kevin decided to join a church nearby and devote his time singing in the choir. He wanted to be a singer – so all he did was sing – rather than looking for a job. He was satisfied living off of and being taken care of by both me and Peter.

However, I was not worried about Kevin. I was free in a whole new world and ready to take it over, too. My job at Sonic Burger Stop was a brainless, monkey type of job. I had fun with my co-workers. We spent more time talking than working. My managers all loved me, so I got away with a lot. I never paid for any meals because I ate while I worked, whenever I got a chance. I was not supposed to be doing that, but I got away with eating for free. Co-workers, management, and customers all seemed to love me.

Whenever I got paid, I gave some of the money to Peter for stuff around the house. Kevin and I used all his household and hygiene products, but Peter seemed okay with letting us using anything we wanted in the apartment. Plus, I suspected Peter was messing around more and more with Kevin. Once I started paying Peter with money, using our bodies as repayment for our debt should have ended. Kevin and I had both agreed not to fool around with Peter anymore. But Kevin didn't stop.

I did not care; I was over Kevin. I was just biding my time to leave Peter's apartment. My plan was to leave both Kevin and Peter to do as they wished without me. I became distrustful of Kevin and realized he was bringing me down. Kevin was only useful for the move to San Antonio, but now that we were out of El Paso, I didn't really need him.

After a month, Peter tried messing with me more. I was not down with that, especially since his hands were all over my 'supposed' boyfriend, Kevin. I knew I had to move out really soon.

I started confiding with one of my co-workers, Terry, about my problems with Kevin and Peter. She was a single, sweet, carefree and caring individual filled with life. Terry was about 5'7" tall, 132 lbs. with ultra-light blonde, curly, shoulder length hair and a light porcelain skin tone. She was eighteen and had dropped out of high school in eleventh grade. Instead of finishing school, she got herself a job and an apartment. She did not own a car yet, because was not able to afford one yet. The bus was Terry's form of transportation.

Terry was lived in a nearby apartment complex. Her rent included all utilities. It was not the best looking place, but nevertheless, it was a place to call her own. Once I got to know her better, I asked if I could move in with her for a while until I found something more permanent. We had become close friends, so she happily agreed.

School was starting again that week. I wanted to register myself. Kevin decided to drop out, since he was already seventeen. Not me; I was not ready to quit school. I knew I had to continue with my education to become the man I wanted to be. I was on a mission to find my true self.

I knew this older, Hispanic lady named Mrs. Johnson. She was a widowed, retired bus driver. Living inside all day kept her complexion pale and wrinkled. Her 5'3" frame rattled around 99 lbs. as she smiled throughout her day. She was a jolly, nice lady that mostly dressed in nightgowns all day. She lived in a house across from the old place I had been living in with Kevin and Peter. Mrs. Johnson pretended to be my grandma to register me for high school in San Antonio. It was an easy sell. In fact, she had very similar short, white, thin hair and gray eyes with those same oval lids as my own granny.

I was excited to be going back to school. The new experience was all possible with the kind help of Mrs. Johnson.

I finally had the courage to break up with Kevin and to find my way through this crazy world. Kevin started crying. "But I'll be all alone," he wept like a baby.

"Sorry, but you are supposed to be my boyfriend. And I know you let Peter do whatever he wants with you behind my back," I said. It wasn't the only reason, but it was the biggest one.

"But I have to," he objected. "Peter makes me do it because I'm not paying rent."

"I'm not going to be anyone's second best. And why am I paying rent for the both of us, anyway, if you're just going to do that?" I was done with Kevin. I grabbed what I could fit in a cardboard moving box, along with the bag I came with from El Paso. I left the rest behind with Kevin. I needed to get out of that place and away from both of those losers; Kevin and Peter.

When I got to Terry's apartment, she had made us a celebration meal with Kool-Aid to drink. She said, "Welcome roommate, get ready for your new start!" That definitely explained what I was going through right then, except I did feel confused about my feelings for Kevin after leaving him. However, I was not about to turn around and go back to that dysfunctional living arrangement. I was ready to move on and live with my friend Terry.

School was fun. New teachers, classes, and new surroundings offered a fresh start. I fit in pretty well, and living with my friend Terry was so fun. We had late night pillow talks and shared our dreams and fears with each other. I was finally able to enjoy living in San Antonio. Terry showed me the different things and places San Antonio had to offer. It was fun sharing those new memories with her.

Only two weeks after I moved out, Kevin decided to call. A lot. He blew up my friend's home phone and talked all kinds of shit. He found out what Mrs. Johnson did for me to get me back in school and thought he could scare me to take him back if he threatened to tell on us.

"If you don't take me back," threatened Kevin, "... then I'm going to let the cat out of the bag."

"You wouldn't dare," I replied.

"Oh yes I would. I will go to your school and tell them that the woman who signed for you is not your grandma, but a neighbor," he said.

"How is hurting me going to make me want you back?"

I asked sarcastically. If Kevin followed through with his threat, that would surely get me kicked out of school. I was not going to allow it.

Kevin was silent on the other end. Just as he was about to speak again, I yelled back at him. "I gave you a break but now you have crossed the line with me, Kevin. Payback is coming to you. And not the way you would like it." Then I hung up the phone before he had a chance to react.

I was determined to mess up Kevin's life. There was pride in his singing voice, so I knew the way to hurt him the most would be to lose his talented vocals. He had a beautiful voice and sang really nice in the church's choir. So, I asked Momo to curse him. It was the first time I had turned to Momo since I moved with Kevin and Peter. "Destroy his voice, Momo. Ruin Kevin's ability to perform as a singer."

Since the move to San Antonio, I never really had the opportunity to be alone to talk to Momo. I started to figure out how to ignore and tune out Momo for several weeks, or perhaps most of the summer. It was not an easy task, but I managed to do it. I knew Momo was not happy being ignored, but was very pleased that I came back to needing him again.

This time, Momo came to me and told me I needed a fresh, new name, which was to be Kris. He wrote it on the restroom window after I had finished taking a shower one morning. I felt it was unique and a name people would not forget. Momo said he always wanted to be with me and felt that we were each other's toy; connected as one. I did not mind the name Kris, especially since I did not like being called Michael. So from that day on, I asked and told everyone I encountered to please call me Kris. Soon, everyone came to know me as Kris.

Not long after summoning Momo, Kevin lost his singing voice. He didn't even try to sing again and then moved back to El Paso with his parents. However, even before all of that took place, apparently Kevin started dating another guy only three days after I moved out; even though he was still trying to get back together with me. I found out what Kevin had been up to after I left him. Some of my friends spied on his social media accounts.

So, I decided to befriend the new guy that Keven was dating, perhaps out of spite. His name was Mark. He was a preppy type of guy. Prior to meeting Mark, I saw some pictures of him online. He was 17 years old, Hispanic, 5'6" and only 112 lbs.; with light brown eyes, olive skin tone, and light brown hair. Indeed, Mark was pretty cute. He was interested in video games, friends, family, shopping, and loved pizza.

In order to get to Mark, I fabricated an online profile. Instead of using my name, Kris, I made up an alias. My alter ego was a total 'goodie two shoes' type of guy that cared about kids and saving the animals.

Using my deviant profile, I started trying to get close to Mark. After a week of chatting back and forth through social media, Mark finally decided to meet me at the mall. Unfortunately, he had no clue that I was the '*ex*' of his new boyfriend, Kevin. I didn't mention it, either. After meeting once, we made a few more dates thereafter.

Mark did tell me he was in a relationship, but he downplayed it. I could tell that Mark was not serious about Kevin. We talked for hours each time we got together. He would stare into my eyes. We held hands. It was strange, but I started to feel a strong connection with Mark and I knew he liked me, too.

It was time for me to get what I wanted. Then I realized I wanted to be with Mark. I stole him away from Kevin, albeit unintentionally. He made me feel different; something I had never experienced before. I felt safe telling him about my life and other deep, personal emotional issues I dealt with.

Eventually, I even told Mark about Kevin. Mark seemed a little bit shocked, but then said he was flattered that I fought for the prize at the end of it all; him. It felt like Mark completed me. My heart yearned for him.

Was I actually was falling in love with this guy? How did this happen to me? I felt like I was always on cloud nine whenever I was with him. Just being close to Mark made my heart skip a beat sometimes. He treated me like a king. If we were not in school or at work, we were together. To say the least, we were inseparable.

Since Momo had recently changed my named, I asked Mark to change his, too, for me. Of course, Mark did not know about Momo yet, but he would soon find out about him.

"I am going to give you a nickname," I told Mark. "We

shall call you Bert. Mark liked that nickname, especially because it came from the show *Sesame Street.* Whenever he saw Bert on T.V. or at a store, he would get so excited and happy. I even bought a small stuffed toy one for him. Mark hugged it all the time while we were at home.

During the days and nights, Bert stayed with me. He washed my clothes and cooked meals. Sometimes he surprised me with breakfast in bed. He left little love notes in places I would find them. When Bert told me he loved me, it felt so right. I did not question anything about that. We were in love – and to the world – we were a team that was unstoppable.

My roommate friend Terry was not bothered that Bert was always over. She said that because he was always cleaning and making meals for everyone, she also felt pampered by him too.

We spent days just laughing and talking about random things. Sometimes we just stared at each other and were fine just doing that. We didn't have to speak. We knew what one another was thinking and we were in sync most of the time. Most nights, Bert fell asleep holding me. I felt like I was the most special person in the world.

Within months, Bert started expressing other things he wanted to do. "I was thinking... I want to dress up like a female impersonator. And I need a girl's name, too."

"How about Dejia?" It was supposed to be Bert's drag name that Momo told me to give Bert. Momo tried to plant a seed in him, but it did not work out as planned. Bert did not like the drag name Dejia.

"Mmmm, I don't think that's really me," said Bert, with a scrunched up nose of disdain. "Do I look like a Dejia? I think not. I shall call my female persona, Trixie!"

Momo did not like the new name, not one bit. As a matter a fact, Momo was furious with both Bert and I for going along with it. He came to me one night and we discussed it. "Bert needs to be punished for going against the name I have chosen," said Momo. "And now it is time for him to meet me."

I was afraid of what Momo would do to Bert just over a name. He did not tell me what he would do to discipline Bert, but based on past experiences; I knew it was not good to make Momo mad.

Up until this point in my life, I had pushed people away, because of the gifts I had. People were so scared of me. But my love, Bert, was not impressed with these abilities. He knew much more about the different people in me. When Bert told me about different encounters, it offered a vivid visualization about the daily life I faced – living in this body – yet, sharing me with Momo and all the others.

Bert also had firsthand knowledge about my healing talents. "Look and observe what I do," I told Bert one day. "I am going to tell you some very specific things that are going on with each person and what will happen to them as a result. Don't worry, they will be happy and fine after this test."

Sometimes, I merely touched their hands. "Wait about a week to see what happens," I told Bert. He witnessed the blessings that I had put upon them, although they were frightened.

Chapter Eight

SEX, MIGUEL AND MONEY

One night, I had a vision that I wanted to become a porn star. I was only seventeen. Now that I was living in a new city and away from my mother, I could be anything I wanted to be.

As a porn star, I needed a stage name. On that day, I reinvented myself as Miguel. Miguel was interesting and sexy as hell. Everyone wanted to know him and wanted him as their arm candy; he was that guy with the physical sex appeal and chiseled great looks. I became Miguel to escape being Michael. My self-esteem rose as Miguel, so from that day on, Miguel came to life and Michael was considered dead.

When Miguel came around, I saw and felt Momo getting jealous of him. Since Momo was in my life for most of my childhood and teenage years, he had directed me how to survive. But Miguel showed me a different way. Momo tried to take control of Miguel. He got mad and the two spent long hours arguing with one another.

Miguel was my inspiration to become a sex symbol and complete the vision of doing porn. Even if I had to sell myself, I would. Whatever it took to become the hottest ass around was my motto. Sex, drugs, and lies were Miguel's tools. He was a compulsive liar and whispered sweet nothings to his listeners' ears. Miguel was a statue and everything he touched was gold.

As the year went on, I developed many connections. People believed that I was twenty-one years old. Sadly, I was just about to turn eighteen. After my eighteenth birthday, I started hanging around people that could make my vision come true. Within weeks, I had two offers to do porn. It was astonishing, but I thought it was my destiny to become everyone's wet dreams.

Miguel was the one who started making me money and paying my bills. He was in full control of anything I did, from my thoughts to my actions. As I started getting my name out there more and more, life became easier.

Miguel chose who he spent time with carefully. He dropped out of school. He believed he had gained all the knowledge he could from such a dreary, mundane institution. He was very street-savvy. He knew how to pull people's strings and give them what they wanted. Money was given to him to start ventures and other profitable events. People did not realize these were all made-up business deals being played on one another for Miguel's personal gain. They never knew how they were being used in his Ponzi game.

People also gave him money just to have him around; whether at parties, events or fund raisers. Just knowing the name "Miguel" made people want to come to the occasion.

Traveling from San Antonio to the cities of Austin, Houston, and Dallas gave Miguel the personification of a successful business man. In reality, Miguel was an opportunist. He was only interested in obtaining wealth, prosperity and fame.

Soon, I was entering bars with people who were very important in the social scene. It gave me 'V.I.P' status. I stayed at any nearby hotel or sometimes even passed out in my car near or at the event.

One night, while at a gay club in Austin, TX, called Ecstasy, there was a men's wet T-shirt stripping contest. The prize was some easy cash. Of course, I entered and did my thing. I told myself in a really low voice – while changing in the back among all the other contestants – *"I got this. I am the shit and everyone is going to love me when I get out there. I will make each and every one in the audience want this bod."*

We all had paper numbers pinned on some part of our clothing. I was officially 'Number 8' in the contest.

I went out on the stage, pushing guys out of my way and dancing in front of other contestants. Whatever it took to show that I was the best on that stage, I made it happen. I shook my ass and dropped it real low; bouncing it up and down so much you would have thought it was moving on its own. The strippers all got wet with buckets of water thrown at us by the crowd. Then, I jumped off the stage to a nearby stripper pole and did a striptease around the pole. It was pretty hot and the fans were screaming for more. After the song was over, I took a bow and rushed back on stage among the losers.

The show organizers finally told the crowd to scream for their winner. The announcer placed his hand over each of the contestant's heads as they walked by to hear the crowd's reaction. We heard some screams for others and then it was my turn. I grabbed my wet underwear, held my cock and screamed, "Miguel baby!" The crowd went wild as hell.

They loved me; I knew they would. The announcer kept going to finish the rest of contestants. Wait, I thought I had already won? As he kept going down the line, there were a couple of cheers and screams but nothing compared to mine.

The announcer said, "We all know who the real winner is tonight!"

"Yeah!" shouted the crowd.

"It's Number 8, Miguel! Come on up here!" I went to the announcer to receive recognition. He stood there talking, while another guy delivered us some liquor shots. "You just won $500 dollars!" Under the screams of the crowd, he said, "Here's a salute to Miguel, Number 8!"

The contestants all drank the shot at the same time. It burned going down my throat and had a strong cinnamon aftertaste. The host grabbed my arm. "Follow me to claim your prize. This way," he pointed, whereupon I was escorted to another level of the club.

Upstairs, there were two, huge, mighty muscle men standing in front of a bold, red wooden door. One of the guys was Hispanic and the other was African American. Both were about six feet tall and pure muscle with no fat, like the bodybuilder types. Neither had facial hair and both were bald. They wore similar, dark blue designer suits. Neither of the two guys smiled nor spoke to me. They maintained a mean and serious look on their faces. The sign on the door read, '*Manager's Office*'.

"This is tonight's stripper winner," the announcer told the guard.

One guard nodded to the other and he proceeded to knock on the door.

We heard, "Enter."

The announcer walked in first, followed by me. He closed door. He said, "Big Daddy Q, here is the winner." He stood me in front of the head honcho. "Sexy, isn't he?"

The guy they referred to as '*Big Daddy Q*' was an older, heavyset guy with a short, black beard and slicked back, black, short, greasy hair. His 5'9" frame stretched thin over his thick muscles, which were tucked neatly into his dark black slacks. Diamonds set in gold rings caught the light in the room and bounced all around like a disco ball. The diamond studs in his ears winked at me. His dark, black eyes sized me up.

Big Daddy Q sat behind his office desk and pointed up

to the monitor over our heads. I looked up and saw a T.V. hanging on the attached wall. "You were pretty good. Entertaining to watch, I must say. I am the manger here at the prestigious Ecstasy club. We only have the cream of the crop in male dancers here. Our high class clientele must be pleased. I am in charge of the attractions here. Now, I'm going to offer you a chance to make extra cash working here as one of our showcase strippers. I think you will bring a Latin spice that we need right now."

He leaned over and reached into the bottom drawer of his desk. Tossing an envelope at me, he smirked. "I took this out of the main safe for tonight. It is your prize for the show you put on."

"Thank you," I replied, picking up the envelope.

He rested his bulky shoulders back against the high, leatherback office chair. "I expected to see you tomorrow night at 9:00 sharp," said Big Daddy Q. "Be ready to meet the rest of the talent here. I suggest you get some hotter underpants and some knee pads to dance around in, for both on and off the stage."

With a smirk, I said, "Thank you for the opportunity. I will think about it."

He looked at me and said, "You have only one chance tomorrow night. Be here if you want the job. You can leave the way you came in." Then, Big Daddy Q looked over my head with a dismissive note to his nod.

As I turned and walked away, he said, "You better think

hard about what I am offering you. Others would give everything to be standing in your shoes."

I looked back at him, as I opened the door and I walked out with my cash in hand. "Okay," I acknowledged.

Walking out of the club, I thought about how I was going to party it up with the prize money. Luckily, having friends with valid license cards over twenty-one was not a problem for me. I could get anything I wanted just by demanding it. I partied the rest of the night until early morning; with a random group of people who were in the club.

The next afternoon, I woke up late in my hotel room. When I looked over to the clock on the bedside table, it was 4:00 p.m. Funny, I didn't even remember driving back to the hotel, but at least I was all in one piece. Looking out the window, I saw my vehicle. It was there and seemed to be okay, too. I took a bath and got dressed. By then, I was super hungry and still felt hungover from all the alcohol I drank the night prior. But I was off to go get something in my empty stomach.

After eating a late breakfast, I went cruising around to get some new, sexy underwear for later that night. I had decided to give the new stripper job a try. So, if I was going to be the latest and hottest Go-go boy at the club, I had to look sizzling hot. I wanted to make all the freaking money.

I found an awesome store in Austin that sold the sexiest male and female stripper clothes. I was in heaven, with all those freaky clothes. I bought so many pairs of underwear and clothing that I couldn't wait to try them on in my hotel right away. Then, I figured I would rest a bit before it was time to go back to the club.

By 8:53 p.m., I returned to the Ecstasy club. A lot of guys were already there, waiting around and talking to each other. I walked in a grabbed a chair in the middle of the mix of guys. Sitting down confidently on the chair, I said, "Hey! I am Miguel. I start tonight. What's up fellas?"

Some returned the '*Hello*', while others shook my hand, and some just kept talking amongst themselves, as if I were not there. But I was not worried about those losers. I knew I was going to get all the money. I was only concerned about making all that money, not about the losers who worked there.

The manager came in with his soldiers (aka – his body guards). Right away, he took charge. "Shut up, guys. We have a lot to go over before the show tonight. First, we didn't hit our liquor sales last night, even with the contest. People also waited a long time for refills and drinks. Some of you Go-go boys took too much time on breaks, instead of keeping the crowd entertained. I am not happy with this shit at all. You know I got cameras up there," he raised his voice and pointed at the ceiling. "And I'm watching you mother fuckers!"

Some of the staff hung their head shamefully. Big Daddy Q wasn't finished. "We have a new Go-go boy to add to our collection here at Ecstasy Club. His name is Miguel. He'll be the Latin flavor to spice things up." He pointed at me. "I want everyone to show him the ropes. Do whatever needs to be done to make <u>me</u> happy tonight. Now, get ready!"

The rest of the night was fascinating. I met a lot of big spenders and great connections. I worked hard and took very few breaks. I wanted to work the crowds, so I roamed around, flirting with any guy that was near. I knew everyone had money to give me. Shots were given to me and to the customers one after another, which made the guys buy more and more. If everyone was drunk, they would all give their money away to me.

Some old farts were touching me and licking my body anywhere they could. It was gross, but I knew as long I was getting big cash, it was okay. "A dollar doesn't get you much," I'd say. "You got to pay if you want this." So, they gave me money left and right.

As I walked away from one old dude, I told him he'd better be waiting for me with lots of money if he wanted more. As long as he was going to give me big money, I didn't mind giving him extra time and rubbing my body all over his.

I was living my dream. By the end of the night, I walked out with $722. I knew I could have gotten a lot more, but I was still learning what I could get away with. The money was there, I could feel it. I just needed to learn how to choose the right ones, so that I would get that jackpot each time.

Of course, some didn't have much, but I took every last dollar they had. Without a question or second thought, these guys gave whatever I told them to give.

The nights following got better and better. I was racking in the cash. It was so easy for me to walk in the club and expect the customers to pay for my attention. There were even guys trying to get in line for my time. I was pretty smooth. They waited for their turn, and had the money ready. My hot ass was right there as soon as I saw the fistfuls of green. They were my puppets.

Finally, I was getting the hang of it. I even learned who paid big and who did not. I did not waste time with the small cash, except maybe a second if I had time to spare in between the bigger fish with lots of cash.

One long, tiring night after I had been working the club for about three months, a guy came in whom I had not seen before. Being 6'2" and white, he caught my eye. He was a typical white guy with his straight, light, blond hair and blue eyes set in pale skin. He took a lingering look at me while I was dancing in a huge, walk-in cage.

"Damn! You are smoking, firecracker hot! You belong in a bigger venue, making more money."

Of course, those words piqued my interest. "Go on..."

"I know this dude that manages a club called '*Luscious*' in Corpus Christi, Texas. He is involved in the porn business from South Beach Miami, Florida. They are looking for fresh, hot guys. You definitely fit that bill."

Now, he really had my attention. "You don't say?"

Then, he said as an afterthought, "By the way, my name is Randy."

Randy appeared to be in his mid-thirties and was dressed up in a classy, black and silver striped pair of slacks, with a multi-color collar polo shirt that brightened his deep, blue eyes. He was a very good looking older man.

"I can take you there, but in return, I must ask that you take care of me tonight." Randy said to me.

I looked at him and said, "You must be fuckin' stupid dude and a brave, cocky asshole to talk to me like that."

Randy looked me up and down and said, "I just did".

I took a step back and took a deep breath. Then, I replied, "I am not doing shit for you for free. Show me the cash and maybe I will let you take me to that supposed club this coming week. You are for sure able to take me to South Beach in Miami, Florida, right?"

"No, the club is in Corpus Christi. But South Beach is where the porn business is." His face lit up with my question. "Filming is for only a select few."

He paid me and I entertained him in between my other big spenders. I had most of them all sharing a booth in the VIP area. I made sure I kept my money close and with easy access to me. That night went by so fast. Before I knew it, closing time was upon us. Randy asked for my number. I gave it to him.

"On Tuesday, which is two days from now, I will call you to meet me in front of this club at 10 a.m.," he instructed. "We leave for the Corpus Christi meeting.

I replied, "Yeah, see you then. And afterwards, you might get a treat for taking me, too."

Tuesday came and I was ready. I headed to the club to wait

for Randy to pick me up. He did not call, nor did I have his number. However, I still waited, by his word at 10:00 a.m. When he didn't show up, I told myself I would only wait another fifteen minutes. Meanwhile, I messed with my cell phone to pass the time.

Suddenly, I heard a car honk. I looked up and it was Randy pulling up to the curb near me. He drove a bright, cherry red, convertible, Ford Mustang GT with a black top. It was an impressive, muscle vehicle and he looked great driving it, too. Without saying anything, I got up and put my bag in the backseat then climbed into the passenger seat. Off we went to Corpus Christi, riding with the top down. It was a fabulous way of transportation for me.

We talked most of the way. He kept the conversation going, asking questions and bringing up topics. I answered and responded accordingly. Finally, we pulled into the Luscious Club's parking lot. I jumped right out of Randy's convertible car, took a breath to steady myself and followed him into the club. I was born ready to do this.

The guy inside was near the bar, drinking a mixed drink. He hunched over some paperwork. He looked up as we walked in. "What's up Randy? Is this the hot little tight snapper you were telling me about?"

Randy nodded. Then the guy addressed me. "They call me Romero. I am the owner of Luscious here in Corpus. I hope you brought your 'A' game to amaze me, little boy."

Romero was an over-the-hill, Latin man in his late

fifties. He sported salt and pepper, short hair. Although he was past his prime, he still tried to act fresh. Romero looked like a drug dealer, with a cell phone on his side and one in front of him, right next to his office phone. He sat in front of a laptop at his desk. His green eyes darted from the screen through the dim light of the room. He had huge diamond and gold rings on most of his fingers and a couple of thick, gold rope necklaces dangling on his neck. These accessories contrasted with his dark skin tone. He was dressed in all black slacks, a black T-shirt, and a black sports coat. You could tell that Romero was full of shit from the minute he opened his mouth.

I said, "I am Miguel from El Paso, Texas. I have been working for months as a Go-go guy in Austin, at a club called Ecstasy."

He turned from his paperwork and said, "Okay, show me what you got? You have one chance to prove yourself to me. How do you feel in your body?"

I said, "It is hot and it makes me money."

"Take your clothes off and show me what you got," Romero instructed.

I looked at Romero and then Randy. They just looked back at me, expectantly. Within seconds, I stripped my clothes off and danced for him. I even jumped on the stripper pole to show him my moves. When I stopped, he said, "Okay. You got it. See you this Friday at 10:30 p.m., ready to go. Do not be late. We have a back locker room for your stuff. Bring a lock. Its employees only back there!"

As I followed Randy out I said, "See you then."

That Friday night, I felt different, like a break was coming. I had a guest spot in the lineup. I was like a special performer; the main act. When I heard my name called by an over-the-top, drag queen announcer, I took a deep breath and ran onto the stage. I did a little dance to a song they played, while people came up to give me dollar bills. It was okay, but I did not see the big funds like in Austin.

"*Maybe I took a wrong move coming here*," I thought to myself. Yet, I sucked it up and took a shot every time I had a chance.

I felt a little bit too buzzed when the manager came out and announced that pictures with strippers were needed. "Get out your $20 dollar bills, because this is your lucky day!" Romero shouted to the audience. "If you want a picture with one of these guys, then get your cash ready!"

A photographer came in to prepare us for some hot business deals. I got in line and took a lot of pictures with clients. They paid simply to get a picture touching me. I knew I had to slow down the drinking and get some water. It was way too early and I had a shortage of money in my underpants, even after that spontaneous photo shoot. I finished the night, but overall it was a bummer going to Corpus Christi.

The next night, I debated on whether to return to Austin or not. I decided since it was Saturday night and I was already there in Corpus Christi, I might as well give it a shot. That night, there was a buzz going around Club Luscious staff members. "I heard that the promoters are coming in tonight to possibly grab some of the strippers for their porn business in Florida," whispered one bartender. Everyone clapped like giddy school chicks.

I was so excited when I heard the news. We all carried on with the night and no one showed up. Just as we all were leaving, the owner, Romero, came out of his office to tell us something. "Listen up! Tomorrow, Sunday, I need all of you to come in at 6:00 p.m. for an hour or so. My partners are flying in from Florida to check you animals out and see if we have some hot studs here for some porn action. They land at three in the afternoon, and I am picking them up from the airport. I will take them to the hotel before coming here to see you guys. Be here tomorrow."

Finally, I was excited again.

That Sunday afternoon, I was ready. I rubbed some oil all over my body to give it a wet, sexy look. I rocked a pair of sexy underwear and was ready to show off my moves to whoever the judges were. I got to the club at about 5:45 p.m. Most of the guys were already waiting there, too. Around 5:53 p.m., a black, stretch limousine arrived. The partners were inside and waited in the parked limo until it was time to check us out.

A huge sex extravaganza of judging was about start. Romero came in first. The judges stood right behind him. He started off by announcing, "It's my pleasure to have these certified experts in the adult film industry here with us tonight. First, let me introduce to you... "Romero looked over his shoulder to see if the models and experts were ready. "Feast your eyes on this gorgeous lady, Hilary Lynn, a former adult film actress who is still in her prime." Hilary smiled when she heard her name.

Romero kept moving through the list. "Next to her stands Carlos, a producer who does not have to look for work. He has worked done projects from A-listers throughout Hollywood and all over the globe. He is the guy men and women go to when they are ready to become famous by acting in his films."

Carlos gave everyone a wave, while Romero revealed another judge. "Last we have the brilliant Bobby, who can spot talent like no other. He knows your strengths even before you discover them."

"Standing in front of you are wild animals; the most elite in the business. Give them all a round of applause for taking time out of their busy schedules to be here with us tonight.

They moved to sit at the long table so they could view each of us, one-by-one. As the group sat down, we got ready for the best performance ever. However, maybe I was the only one, but I was not so impressed. To me, I saw a very different group.

For one... Hilary looked like an old, tired out supermodel; minus all that money. No one dared say it, but we all knew that she was not pretty anymore. She had bleach blonde, long, thin, frizzy hair, blue eyes, and very pale, dry skin. Hilary slapped on tons of makeup, which made her look like the grim reaper as a female. Her short, red dress was supposed to be tight and form-fitting, but on her; it looked like she needed to eat more. The gold heels gave her the resemblance of a retired prostitute from before Christ.

Next to her was Carlos, a dark, black, short man. He was bald and clean shaven at forty-something. His brown eyes squinted with every smile. Out of the three, Carlos was the friendliest. He had a smile on his face every time I looked at him.

Bobby was a pretty, young guy of about 25. At 5'11", Bobby's frame looked like a surfer dude. His blue eyes and tanned skin were framed by short, curly, brown hair streaked with blonde highlights. He had no facial hair either, but kept tossing his short hair back and forth as though he had recently cut it. As soon as he sat down, Bobby demanded the drinks. "Keep 'em flowing," he yelled to the bartender.

All I could think about was this lousy drunk getting the beer goggles ready for the judging. I needed a plan quick, so I decided to step up my game. I shouted, "I got the drinks."

Right away, I heard the drink orders coming from each of the judges. I handled them myself and went behind the bar counter to prepare and make them drinks. I had made drinks before, so no one really stopped me. I finished and pranced back to their table, whispering in Bobby's ear first. "I cannot wait to play with you later, hot stuff." Then, I put his drink down in front of him.

Carlos had ordered a double shot. As I set his drink down on the table in front of him, I leaned in to whisper in his ear. "I am ready to be tasted if you like."

With a sultry turn, I was almost sitting on Hilary's lap. I winked at her and said, "How we are supposed to work when we have a sexy distraction in front of our eyes. I would love to be in a movie with you, foxy."

Then, I hurried backstage to get dressed into my show outfit. My goal was to steal the film role right out from under those idiots and losers who were trying to compete on the same stage with me.

My chosen outfit was a see-through, black, long sleeve, form-fitting, dressy shirt, with red thong underwear that had enough room for my shaft to be flopping all around for everyone's pleasure.

When it was my turn, I danced right along to the song. I used the dance pole and even did a move on the pool table. I made sure I kept giving them all eye contact at different times of my performance. I unbuttoned my see-through shirt slowly to work them up. I licked my lips, winked, touched and grabbed all over my body as much as I could. I grabbed a chair from right next to their table. Using it as an object prop was pure genius. I did a lap dance on that empty chair, but I pretended someone was on it. I never lost attention to the detail of the performance I gave them. I had an exotic, sex appeal with intense energy. I was Miguel. After I was done, I went back in line to wait with the rest of the guys.

My heart was beating triple times faster than normal. I was so excited to have this opportunity that grabbed it by the balls. I knew I would be chosen. They all wanted me; I could feel it. I was going to win. Some of the competition had a hot body or looks, but I had it all; body, looks, and the moves that made them come to the yard. It was me they all wanted.

Finally, after all of the contestants had their chance to take the stage in front of the porn panel film company, Carlos, the producer, stood up and said, "We are going to go into the office and discuss who we want, as well as the terms and conditions of filming with our agency. Get out of here and enjoy the rest of the night, fellas. A select few of your lives will change and become stars with us. I mean... MAJOR STARS! See you later."

We heard them talking about us as they were escorted to the manager's office. Everyone else left. However, I wanted to stick around and make sure I was picked. I was willing to go the extra mile to get in. But the bouncer refused me. "You have to leave too, little man." He said, as he directed me out of the club.

I returned to my hotel to wait and see what would happen. The next day, I got a call from the manager. He wanted me to come in around 3:00 p.m. to talk. I calmly agreed to the time. After I got off the phone, I screamed so loud with excitement. I knew I had it in the bag. I was going to be a star and make some crazy, large sums of money.

On my way to the club, I thought about all the things I would buy and how I would spend the money. I wanted to buy an expensive, two-story house; with lavish furniture all through it. It must have a pool in the backyard, too. I wanted a sporty, red convertible Lexus and a black Mercedes Benz. I wanted gold and diamond jewelry to wear with my designer outfits. I could hardly wait.

When I got to the club, the manager was waiting in the dance hall. He told me, "Take a seat in my office and I will be right in. Security will be waiting for you while I get a drink. Do you want one too?"

I said, "Yeah. Vodka with a splash of sprite and a lime."

He turned to the bar and said, "Cool see you in a minute."

When I walked into his office, I noticed there were some pictures of me on his desk. They were enlarged to 8" x 10". They were from the photo shoot a couple of nights before. Everything clicked in my head. A lot of money was riding on this deal; that is why the manager rushed me to become a part of it. I sat down while I waited for him; just looking at my pictures spread all over his desk.

When Romero returned with a drink, I said right away, "So what kind of cash figures am I going to make and how soon?"

Taken aback, he replied, "Whoa! Slow down, cowboy. I will handle this meeting, not you, pretty boy. First of all, I want to make sure you are well taken care of by us. Save your questions until I am done speaking. I have talked to my partners in the porn industry and they certainly want to get you in their film productions."

Then he pushed a paper on a clipboard in my direction. "Here is the contract we have created for you. I need you to sign it within a couple of days. Then we will discuss your flight and hotel stay; all paid by us while you are shooting the films. You got any questions, now is the time to ask."

"Hell yes, I have lots of questions. Give me a few minutes to read this contract," I said, sipping my cocktail. I skimmed through the contract. "Let me first start by asking once again – what cash figures am I going to make – and how fast? It states a total of $8,000 for three films, but I only get 50%, which is $4,000. You keep saying '*films*' which means more than just one, so how many am I supposed to be in after these three? What state or cities are these going to be filmed in? Is the wardrobe going to be supplied and a dressing room, too? What about meals during my stayover, wherever I will be? Am I doing the fucking, getting fucked or both? To sum it up, that means I will only be making about $1,333 per movie. To top it off, this contract states that you are also my manager in this and get the other $4,000 for half of my work."

Romero was not happy with my questions, I could tell. He stopped and looked at the paperwork in front of him. He fumbled to say, "This is the best deal I could get for you. You are barely making dollars here and were not making much more working in Austin, so I see this as a jumping point for your film career. Everyone has to pay their dues before making the major money. You're getting $4,000 cold hard cash right away after you finish all three films in two cities surrounding Florida. After only a week of filming. You will be the bottom on the first film, with a black guy. This is his picture." He held it up to show me. All I could see was the massive, hard, black cock.

Then he stated, "After that, they will see if you will do other positions. It all depends on their stories and what they match you up with. Each movie will require a day or so of filming, so be ready to fly back with that cash on your last shoot."

I wasn't sure if I liked the sounds of the deal. I sat there for a minute, trying to take it all in.

"It takes time and patience to get to the top of a career, especially in this business. I know I can get you there, and with more money for the next deal I get for you." He sat back in his fancy chair, with his hands crossed over his head.

I did not need much time to think about it. "No way! It's so ridiculous if you think I am going to sell myself for the world to see for only chip of the proceeds made from these so called three films. I know I am in demand and can get a lot more in my pocket out of this deal. Something is not adding up and I smell greedy people all in the mix."

I tore up the contract and stood up. The security guard was right there to grab me and push me back down in my seat. I shrugged my shoulder to get away from him and looked back to Romero.

Romero said, "I thought you were ready to make

money, was I wrong?"

"No, it is that I am smarter than the other idiots you have been making money off. I am out of here." I stood to go again and the security guard gripped my shoulder again. "Let me go, you big green mile stunt double."

The manager said, "Throw this trash out with the garbage."

While I was being pulled out by my arm, I screamed, "Ha! You are the one that has to tell them the deal fell through with me."

I could not believe that shit. I was so upset. I did not know what to do now. Those cockfuckers were not going to make a dime off of me. I got back home and drank some beer and fell asleep on the couch. I woke up thinking, *'I need to make some money quick to pay bills now that I quit that shit hole. What do I do now?'* Suddenly, I remembered a few of the people I had been chatting with on social media outside Texas.

It was time I started working my magic; focusing on money for sex. What else could I do to make quick, large sums of cash and get gifts too? I contacted ten of them to see which person would pay the most. '*Sex and the company of my time anywhere for money in return*'.

Whenever I prostituted, I went out of town where nobody knew me or would recognize me. It was never with anybody in San Antonio or Texas. During the multiple times I sold my body, it was only with two different men and a woman; all older individuals. These were my three primary clients; however, there were other '*no sex*' encounters in between.

Miguel was a very secretive person. He did things without anyone seeing. He was definitely a star fucker, like a damn great mix drink shot.

To be someone successful, I talked to the people who were somebody. I knew if I was surrounded by successful people, I would be successful in return. I gave these affluent people my business card and made deals with them. In the deal, there were specific details of what I would do for them and what things I would not do. We settled on a price and then traveled to their state during those dates. A prepaid card was sent to me in advance so that I could book my plane tickets. Once I received the prepaid card, I booked my ticket for the flight to and from their location and city.

I also went to a website for people with fetishes or who wanted very little in return for a big payday for me. It was usually guys that were incapable of moving too much, such as those in a wheelchair. They wanted me to walk around in just my underwear around them. The first requirement was that I got paid in cash right when I arrived at their home. If they had gifts for me or took me out for a shopping spree, that was an added treat.

My favorite client was a man named Rudy who resided in Washington. He was the principal of a middle school and the most demanding of all three clients. He was married, with a wife and five kids aged between 18 to 33 years old. At 230 lbs.,

Rudy was overweight for his 5'8" frame. His olive, wrinkled skin showed his 61 years. His glasses made him look like an old man pervert. He mostly wore a baseball cap outside of work.

Rudy had several vehicles, including a baby blue, Jaguar F-Coupe. It was the sweetest and most expensive car I had ever driven. I drove around in it while visiting his city. He was my prince charming – minus the looks – of course. His pockets were fat with abundant cash at my disposal when I played my cards correctly with him.

"Be a good boy," Rudy often told me. He had a weird father and son fetish. And he was very obsessed with me. I had to be drunk every time we fucked around. Most of the time, I was grossed out. The money and gifts was the only thing that kept me excited while his filthy hands and body were touching mine.

The charge was settled after careful negations between us. He paid $700 for only one hour, twice a week. Plus, I always had new jewelry that Rudy bought for me, like yellow gold-filled diamond necklaces, bracelets, pendants, rings, earrings, shoes, coats, clothing, and electronics. He took me on shopping sprees to spend more time with me.

Rudy loved making me smile. He'd say, "Looking at you gets me so excited and makes me happy to shower you with these gifts." He took me to a variety of expensive, upscale restaurants that I had never been to yet in my life. Rudy wanted to show me the world and of course show me off as his to the world, too. Just having me escort him to a place made him feel very important. I called him '*Daddy*' but I could tell the store employees or waiters helping us did not believe that Rudy was really my father. I didn't mind, because I made him spend the money before his hour of vomit sex even started.

When we shopped, money was not a limit. "Just pick what you really want and need," he'd say. My list was never complete and sometimes he found what I wanted at a way cheaper cost than what I saw it for. Unless it was too excessive, Rudy usually made it happen.

The most expensive thing Rudy ever bought me was a convertible, silver Mustang GT of the current year. It was custom ordered online to my preferences, and with his approval next to me at the dealership. The total package price came out to $37,666.

"Oh my, it is gorgeous!" I shrieked, still disbelieving that Rudy would willingly give me that much cash to buy my dream car. I thought he was going to buy it under his name and then take it back if I messed up.

"Are you putting the car in your name so that you have something to hold over me?" I asked. I brought it up repeatedly, still not trusting that someone would give that much money without insurance of getting their fair share back from a person. Well to my astonishment, Rudy took me to his bank and helped me open a checking account. He told the bank to transfer $38,000 to my $0 balance, which was enough to cover the purchase of the car and have a few hundred dollars left to spare.

I could not believe my bank deposit receipt. I kept staring at it. Wow! Rudy actually did exactly what he told me he would do. I was in pure shock and so pleased. For some reason after that act of giving and trust, I started liking him. I guess it was because he treated me so good and wanted to give me the world. I wished I could have done it sooner or showed him that I really did care, instead of just using Rudy. I kept that bank deposit receipt for a long time.

During that time of my life, I started developing a very bad, unhealthy, eating disorder. I dropped more weight and starved myself to be skinnier. I worked out at the gym every day and rarely missed a workout for at least one or two hours. For some strange reason, I thought I was fat, even though I was already skinny. My body was not handling the strain on it. I started feeling weak at times during the day. Different parts of my legs or arms fell asleep, even while I was still awake. I managed not to be hungry and sometimes didn't eat anything all day except a soda or small bag of chips.

My health worsened as I started getting dizzy spells, with links of small blood spots of coming from inside my butt hole. I knew this was harming me, but I was determined to be as thin as possible. Rudy told me how concerned he was about my continued weight loss. My rib cage was exposed and my body looked so frail. He wanted me to go to a doctor as soon as possible to make sure I was alright.

"I'm fine and feel great," I brushed him off. "And I look

spectacular." I knew I was only fooling and hurting myself by continuing living like this. Rudy's suggestion stayed heavy on my mind. When I saw more blood than normal coming out, I knew I had damaged my body. I then got so scared about my health status. I decided that I needed to regain control and start eating again to get out of the red alert, deadly zone.

And I wasn't the only one having health issues. One afternoon, I got a call from Rudy. "Listen, I just had a doctor's visit and the clinic has some concerns," he said woefully.

"Like what? Is everything okay?" I was genuinely concerned. But for some reason, Rudy didn't want to share more of whatever was really going on with his health. "It's probably nothing. I'm going back to a follow-up of the tests later in the week. I can't see you until after the appointment."

"Are you sure?" I asked again. I tried hard to get a solid answer and was mostly concerned about whether I would see him again and get my next allowance.

"Don't worry," he replied.

The following week, he called again. It was bad news. "I'm being admitted to the hospital," explained Rudy. "I have cancer and they have to remove the lump quickly. I have to get an operation. But I promise, after this is all done and I have time to heal, we'll get together again."

"I'm sorry to hear this," I said.

"I know," said Rudy. He sounded worried. "Please pray for me and be patient for our love."

I did not know what to do. I felt my heart being ripped

into pieces. A feeling I had never felt before for Rudy came over me. I cared.

Days and weeks passed. Finally, a month after the procedure, I decided to call Rudy. I did not wait for him to contact me. Unfortunately, his wife answered. "My husband told me somewhat about you. Days prior to his first doctor's visit – when he found out about the cancer – Rudy advised me that he was leaving me and our children to be gay and be with you, his younger lover. We were going to sell the house and separate all of the possessions we owned. But that has all changed now," she said coldly. "So, do not bothering trying to get ahold of Rudy, ever again. Leave us alone!"

Then, the phone went to a dial tone. I never spent an hour or even a minute ever again with that dear man. His cell phone number was changed and he disappeared swiftly out of my life.

Ruben was the insurance agent I met in Nevada. We agreed on a set rate of $600 for one to three hours, plus expenses, per visit. I was alright with that because Ruben promised to get me into a lot of the clubs I had not been able to see before. Ruben loved to party in the club scene and was all about the night life. He was a huge alcoholic drinker and loving family man, especially when it came to his parents' well-being.

The first day he picked me up from my hotel, Ruben brought a case of beer for us to drink while we drove around on our way to the club. We drank one beer right after another, and quickly. Each beer disappeared into just a crushed can he threw into a bag in the backseat of his jeep.

Ruben's hands were all over me quickly. Within seconds, his hand was all over my thighs. I was not old enough to drink yet, but that did not stop him from letting me drink or get into the club. He was a smooth talker and slipped tip money to the door bouncers to get us right in. He seemed like the type of guy I would have dated, especially if he were younger. Regardless, we had a lot in common. At least, Ruben made me believe that we did.

As we progressed in the relationship, I didn't know how he got us home safely each time I went out with him to the bars and clubs, after drinking uncontrollably. He did, though. Ruben was able to drive us both back home to our own separate places.

Ruben did not like other men trying to talk to me or showing interest in me. He wanted me all to himself. He knew I was his hoe. When we were at the clubs or bars, random men asked to buy me a drink or dance with me. I learned fast to avoid them and to say no right away and ignore them while Ruben was around. I could tell it really bothered him and I caught him just staring at me with his black, intense, suspicious eyes. He kept a very close tab on every move I made. It made me feel uncomfortable at times, but he was paying me, so I had to suck it up as all business.

Whenever I left him after our dates, I always felt I was being stalked. If I went out in public in Nevada, I saw a similar car drive past me. The driver had short, black, hair like Ruben's. He seemed to be everywhere. I saw his clean shaven, tanned, Hispanic skin everywhere. He tried showing up unannounced at my hotel to see me on an unscheduled date. Most of the time, I didn't go out with him because I started feeling claustrophobic and followed. I became subconscious of my surroundings. I saw Ruben everywhere. When I confronted him, Ruben always made excuses as to why he was there at that exact location. Since he seemed to always be in the same area, after a while I ignored his phone calls if I didn't feel like being pestered.

With Ruben, I did not even feel comfortable going shopping for extra gifts from him. So, that stopped real soon. It was 'pay first' and then I set the timer. It seemed to take forever sometimes. He wanted to know too much about my personal surroundings back home and everyday routines. He definitely knew how to make me feel uncomfortable and gave me creepy vibes. I had to end and cut the ties of that crazy man before it was too late.

Then there was the lovely Ariel. She was a Geometry course high school teacher from Florida. On one of my first trips to see her, I called her the '*lonely explorer*' because she loved to live this romantic lifestyle, even though I was hired as her escort. Ariel was a full-figured woman. Her green eyes contrasted with her Latino complexion. Her bouncy curls hung to her shoulders and swayed with each lively step.

Due to her finances at the time, we settled on $500 per

session. They were to last at least an hour or two each time. She loved taking me to ballets, theatre plays, fancy black tie events, and quiet, secluded, upscale restaurants. Ariel paid extra to get total privacy to flirt back and forth with each other while at restaurant. Champagne and wine flowed constantly and she often put the bottle on the table next to us as a code to bring another bottle quickly. She barely ate while she was with me. Ariel just wanted to kiss and cuddle while we were at the restaurant.

On one of my "off duty" nights, I wanted to explore by walking the area around the hotel I was staying at, since I had never been to this part of Florida. It was around 3:33 a.m., so there was no traffic or vehicles driving in the street. A calm, still, wind of the morning darkness offered a strange feeling.

Suddenly, I swore there was a man staring at me. As I walked around, I felt an eerie feeling way down in my gut. It was fear. But why did I feel this way? As I walked around the empty streets, I heard a noise of movement. There were steps coming quickly behind me. I stopped and turned right around to see who was coming in my direction. In the distance, a dark shadow of a tall man wearing a black cowboy hat and long, thin, black trench coat.

When I turned to see who it could be, he stood still on the corner of the street; only a short block away from where I stopped to stand and look. "Hello!" I screamed out to him. There was no response. "Hello?" He remained stoic and kept staring at me.

The hair on my neck stood up. Chills overcame my body. I was frightened of this man that seemed to be staring and watching me. '*What does he want?*' I wondered. '*Why is he doing that? And what is he getting out of this by spying on me?*'

I started walking faster, but as I took about seven steps, I was now very curious what he was really doing. I had to know, so I turned back around to speak to the guy. But he was gone. There was no one in the streets, they were empty. I started second-guessing myself. '*What was that? Was it really a man?*'

As I started walking back to my hotel, I realized the shadow person had acknowledged me. I felt like he was the devil communicating with me. I went straight to my room, frightened. I was unable to fall asleep right away. I never found out what he wanted from me. All I know is that he was surely interested in me for some reason.

I wondered if maybe Momo had something to do with that shadow man. I knew he wanted me to experience pain for not obeying him. I certainly hoped that I would never see that shadow man or cross his path again.

Having sex with Ariel was one of the hardest things I had to force myself to do. For some reason, I was unable to perform all the way. I usually made sure she was taken care of. I pretended to be sexually aroused and enjoying myself with her during this sex trade. All of my orgasms were fake with her, every time. After several escorting dates, I stopped responding to her request for my services. The money was not worth it anymore and neither was she, in my opinion.

By this time, I had everything I thought I wanted. Youth, a great body, money, sex whenever I wanted it, a sports cars and the fun of traveling from state to state, all on other people's dimes, not mine. However, I felt like something was missing. I had a lost feeling and sense of loneliness. I had achieved so much in such a short period of time, but everyone around me seemed like they were on lesser paths.

I was consumed with my inner demons and Momo was not happy with me at all. I began to ignore him more and more. He told me I would regret doing that, but what could he possibly do to me? Especially since he needed me, rather than the other way around.

So, Momo came to me and whispered in my ear to kill myself. He reminded me that I had made a deal with the devil and he was never was able to claim his prize; my soul. He told me I would have to pay for the wishes that had been granted upon me.

Upon hearing this, I thought to myself; '*Am I really going to hurt myself? Is he going to take my life in some way?*'

There was no way. Momo wasn't crazy enough to get rid of me, was he? But when I turned the lights off, all I heard was his is voice, repeatedly chanting: "Die Bitch, Die Bitch, Die Bitch, You Must Die!" Anger had officially overcome him.

One late, full, moonlit night, I went out clubbing from bar to bar; getting messed up drunk. I was lost in my head and wanted the entire world to stop. I was done living and wanted to end everything. I was tired of people talking about me, hearing them say whatever they wanted to make me feel worthless, making fun of me, saying I was all hype, or thinking I was all that. Momo came into my car and sat in the passenger seat. "You know, Miguel, I think it is time to give in. We both know that you want to die and end it. Just let go and jump out of the car," he dared.

I started crying even more. "Momo, you are right. No one understands me. I am a laughing conversation to people."

Momo turned to me and said, "Just jump, do it now... jump!"

I unclicked my seat belt and jumped out of the moving car. I had been driving about 35 mph on the access road, which was less than six minutes away from my apartment. My car smashed into a nearby tree. My body flew out of the car, rolling to the side of the road. Luckily, it was grassy area with a hill that sloped down to more grass and a metal fence. My body rolled and rolled. I stopped at the fence. I laid there for a couple of seconds before getting up and limping home away from the crime scene.

Fuck, I was drunk and almost killed myself or someone else too. What was I thinking? I realized that Momo indeed wanted me dead and he was not giving up until I was six feet underground. Damn, what a messed up night. I did not even care about the car. The following sunrise, I reported it stolen over the phone. This was after getting up and washing my mouth out from smelling like a bar.

"We'll keep an eye out for it," the police told me. "Someone will get back to you as soon as we find out any information."

Chapter Nine

RIDDLE ME KRIS

Who was really the person behind the phenomenon named Kris? After high school, I was still performing at the clubs and jetting off to dates in other places. I also made grand appearances for cash by promoting different clubs or events. I had a powerfully creative life, winning many awards and being seen by the public. The pushed the envelope on projects as much as possible. I was a multitalented dancer, designer, performer and promoter. I loved the fact that I was involved in working for so many charitable organizations, including child abuse prevention. Companies and people wanted to know me because I was taking over lots of events.

From the clothes I wore and performances that were hyped to the max, people asked, "What is the deal with Kris and when is he going to just fade the hell out?" But I was not a trend. I was KRIS, the real deal. I made the crowd sweat as they moved their bodies along with me. The entertainment I gave them was priceless. It touched hearts.

I was told by many fans that I was almost immortal. It was a spiritual encounter that came alive on stage. I wanted the audience to feel every emotion I gave them while performing. However, I did not allow myself to have real emotions. My expressions and feelings were hidden to everyone off the stage. Yet, I was popular with the people. Kris was a lovable character.

Then, Momo created a stain in his latest plot to take over more of me. He wanted full control of me. Momo wanted to take over my mind, thoughts, actions, body and even my soul to become his puppet. I was not strong enough to fight Momo, so I gave in to him and became Kris. Momo created Kris for his sense of pleasure and amusement. Kris came from the movie character Woody in Toy Story – one of his friends – and of course the doll was also a toy.

Momo and Kris were simply objects. Momo was nothing more than a possessed doll and Kris was vulnerable enough to be molded into anything Momo wanted. The Devil transformed into anything he wanted; through Momo. Therefore, I knew too much and did not even understand the power I possessed through Momo.

As Kris, I was always happy. My symbol was a happy face. I had asked to be happy; that was my wish from the Devil.

As I looked back upon it, Kris was the happy that I asked for from the Devil. It all came together, like a puzzle, piece by piece. Although I saw things clearer, it was too late to stop.

I showed people I was ambitious and successful. It was all a lie, because Kris was running away from what he owed. My craft was of a perfectionist when it came to entertaining fans. But it was hard to find out who Kris really was. Kris, my persona, did not want his story to be told.

Momo kept certain things in the dark so that no one would ever know, including outsiders. The power he had on others was too powerful and everyone was scared to betray his trust or to see Momo come back. He didn't want anyone to know too much, because he thought people would not believe him. He wanted people to see him in person. Not to hear him over a phone or by text.

Sometimes it was hard to bring things from the darkness into the light, because people were afraid of the truth. Once it was revealed, there was no turning back or deleting it. Momo scared me at times, because he showed me things I didn't think existed in this life; yet I have seen them with my own eyes.

For example, there were moments when I caught myself in thought and wondered what made certain things, people, or occasions cross my mind? The more I thought about it, nothing truly existed unless they were put into thought. And so I questioned why these things had manifested. Did a person with very huge meaning in my life cause these thoughts? The question remained a mystery, until the party who created the riddle resolved it.

> *"I can see your thoughts are always important in every way. You can only help and wonder why things cross your mind. The answers to most of our questions are delightfully easy. We obviously do not comprehend these methods. Sometimes it takes digging under the dirt to find the simple answer that worries us. It does not matter whether they are good or bad thoughts, all we can honestly do is take it for what it is. Life is full of disturbance and we can only do so little to ignore it. Yet, disturbance happens every day of our lives. It is one of those thousands of things life puts in our way so we may become stronger; so we may find our power, face our fears and defeat the challenge life offers. We are like birds. We build our lives just like they build their nest."*

Kris often spoke to me in my mind and I wrote down what he was saying. I tried to answer the questions he presented, but I could not. The complexities were too smart for me. Suddenly, Kris's voice disappeared from my head.

I often mulled over the riddles in questions. While being under the influence of drugs and sometimes alcohol did not change the fact that I was dealing with these complicated matters entirely by myself; it was all about that mystery that was still unresolved. My desire to want someone to break this case, my case, and to answer all of my riddles was key. I wanted the voices to stop from taking complete control over me. I wanted to be the leader in every mission in my life. Hence, I left everyone pebbles and crumbs, until one day someone was able to figure out the riddle and get through to me.

It was all part of a game called life. I wondered if there was some higher moving presence moving the pieces of a game in different directions, like chess. Sometimes that higher power put people – either negative or positive – into my life so that a part of the riddle was answered. Sometimes there were road blocks, but then I was lucky enough to find a detour to keep moving on forward. The bigger mystery was; who was really controlling us from another world?

People sometimes asked me or got upset with me about playing games with them. I always told them I was not playing around with them, but I knew that it was really Momo right there, with his hands in the mix. He liked to mirror things out. He made assumptions or little comments, but never said what he really wanted to say.

While I was promoting a show at the club, I had a vision. What if we did Magic Miguel mixed with Burlesque? I wanted everything to be classy, with a dress code. It would be for all sexes and genders – whatever sexual preference you liked. They would come together to experience a show like no other.

How would I describe myself as an entertainer? I was a

good actor. People told me what they wanted me to do and I did it. My appearance was always on point. The outfits that I performed in were futuristic and original, crafted with my own hands. I was a creative creature that expressed my talents through many different, artistic ways. My costumes were something most performers could not pull off and feel great waring. I made the clothes, costumes, and outfits myself. The ideas that I came up with were like plain crayons box blended into a rainbow of colors. I brought color and love to everything I created. I made magic right in front of everyone's eyes. It was a spectacular event each time I performed. I wanted all of my fans to walk away entertained and excited about what I just brought to them. It was like no other, because my talent came from feelings.

> *"We do not grow absolutely, chronologically. We grow sometimes in one dimension, and not in another; unevenly. We grow partially. We are relative. We are mature in one realm, childish in another. The past, present, and future mingle and pull us backward, forward, or fix us in the present. We are made up of layers, cells, constellations."*

As I tried to solve the riddle of "Who is Kris?" it was determined that Kris was an alter ego that I found in myself. Kris was not a non-fictional character, but rather the other person within me. Kris was a real person who had one of the most shocking childhood stories on the planet.

The nickname "Kris" related to me as something special given to me by a loved one. His personality was cute, playful and sociable, just like a favorite toy in Toy Story. Kris was a name associated with happiness.

Chapter Ten

PENNY JUKU VS. KRIS

In order to conceal my identity, I sometimes impersonated a girl. There were vague moments when Penny Juku popped into my head. She came around when I started performing as an entertainer. Penny Juku was a Chinese lady of about 23 years old. She had a pale complexion, was nearly 5'5" tall; 117 lbs. with a slender frame. Her face was made up with a white base and black eye liner; with small, red, heart-shaped lips almost like a mime. She wore Japanese Kimonos that were bright and customary.

Penny Juku was Kris's only personal designer. She gave him her style for the costumes he wore on stage. It was a distinctive Asian style mixed with a bit of Kris.

She was Kris's servant. She dressed him up for the stage shows. She made accessories to match the style of the costume.

She used masks to spice up and cover his face. The masks resembled clown masks that hung on the wall. Penny Juku was no longer a person, but the masks of Kris's true feelings. She was there to protect him and keep him separated from others. Wearing those masks, he felt safer.

Penny Juku wrote down her feelings. It was like a diary, except it was random journaling:

"I, Penny Juku, used to think Kris was wonderful. He was so eager to mold me into being better at everything; when I was on stage with him. I trusted Kris with all my secrets and talents. However, after working for him for five long years, I realized Kris only cares about himself; he used me to the fullest.

For instance, I rushed to help him prepare lines or teach him the choreography for each performance. He has no sense of style or stage presence. He has no rhythm. He does not know how to move his body. I taught him all of these qualities. After many draining, long, horrible hours of being with him – and teaching him dance steps in front of mirrors, or telling him what to say or do in his ear – he finally became the star. He asked me to make all his outfits, both on and off the stage.

My time is valuable and means a lot to me. Kris took both me and my talent for granted. Furthermore, Kris is nothing more than a copycat. There is nothing original about that man. I mean... not a damn thing.

Kris gets me so upset, sometimes by pretending to be my friend, when really he is only interested in what he can gain from the friendship. Very manipulative. Well guess what? Grow up, Kris!

It is strange, but Kris turns into anything he sees coming to life. And if I were to recreate it again, the next time, I'd make it way better. I create camouflage and disguise Kris to blend in with his surroundings. Despite my best efforts, he continues to stand out.

When the smoke clears, all you see is his shadow. I am nobody while Kris is still alive. He makes me stand and wait for his next change, like some idiot. I'll show you who the real idiot is. I can't believe I wait in the dark for him. Everything has to be all about Kris. This is so overwhelming to me. I can't live this way anymore. I want out. Set me free."

A few passing days later, Penny Juku marked another entry:

"I made Kris who he is, but I do not get any credit. I helped him become what everyone now sees. Without me he was lost. He was nothing. He is really my puppet. It is time for me, the real star, to come out and be in the spotlight. Kris is such a huge joke. I am the real performer and everyone is going to know that these are my moves he has been using. I want Kris gone. I need him to fade away.

I remember when I first met him; he was cutting clothes out of blankets and probably his mom's big clothes. I want him to expire; his time is up."

The hatred and tone in Penny Juku's journal entries worsened:

"How am I going to get rid of him? I hate Kris and all that he represents. When he talks to me, I want to spit at him.

I keep lying to myself that I am happy. I am not happy. No way; no how. I do not have a choice with him. I am going to take him over. He needs to move on. I am the ruler and winner in this match. I am taking his place. Then everyone will bow down to the queen.

Everything is wrong here. This life under Kris's thumb is one I wish I could evaporate. He has not treated me right in years. He's going down in flames. Now, everyone will have their chance to see the real Kris as a fake; plastic made into what I wanted him to be. Now, I want nothing to do with him. He will be dismissed.

Let us see how far he goes without my flavor helping every step of the way. I am going to rule this world and take all his fans away. There is only one real talent; the one with the full package. Here I am, Penny Juku, the real star of this show."

Chapter Eleven

DIARY OF A BETRAYED WOMAN, KIKI

One early morning, the air was a bit breezy. I woke up in a panicked state and everything seemed very unfamiliar. I looked all around and noticed that I was in a dark stairway of a parking garage. I did not know how I got there or why I was wearing a very blonde long wig and tight female clothing. I felt so disoriented and confused. I was badly hurt and dirty. It looked as though I had fallen down, since my right knee was bruised and bleeding from a big cut.

I started to see a flashback. The day before, I remember being in my room, watching a story on the T.V. that got my attention. After a while, I glanced toward my balcony, where I sometimes sit outside my apartment. I saw a pink diary book with rhinestones all over it. But whose was this?

I picked it up and started reading the diary. I became immersed in it immediately. It read:

2/2/2014. 1:25 A.M.

"Dear Diary, my name is Kiki and I think my husband Albert is having an affair. I want this not to be for real and to just be my stupid imagination. But my 'guilt' trigger keeps telling me otherwise. I love him with all my heart and do not know how I can FIX this.

I have been so confused these past several months. Albert is supposed to be my loving, devoted husband. And as I write today I do not even know where he is right now or when will he be coming back home to me. I keep thinking in my head, what did I do wrong to keep pushing my husband away?

My eyes are so heavy from crying tears of a lifetime of pain and struggle from deep inside them. I wanted to figure out what journey Albert must be going through to leave me like this. What could have happened to my passionate lover and once best friend? Maybe it was the death of his grandmother that he loved so dearly, his dad's abandoning him as a young boy, alcohol abuse, heart illness, feeling loneliness, another woman or even depression? What had he really been dealing with?'

I started trying to think of all the possible reasons to unfold his story. I must try to get my husband through this, for the both of us. I know I can do this. I can fix any problem... That's me, 'Mrs. Fix It'. There is not a problem that anyone can bring to me that I cannot fix. I have always been the one who figures out what steps to take to get things right again after they go wrong. All problems have a fixable solution; this is what I have always had to do. Especially with the people around me that matter most.

3/16/2014. 4:36 P.M.

To best explain what is weighing on my heart is that if I lose my husband, then emotionally, how can I go on? How could I maintain my sanity? If I only knew, I could have fixed everything. Instead, I was left in the dark.

Who do you trust in your time of need? Who do you turn to? Today, I still do not know who to believe or what really happened.

4/28/2014. 2:19 A.M.

I am going to start writing in this diary; all my everyday thoughts and trials I'm going through. My highs and lows during these trying months will be written into my diary."

"I was left there, standing strong, waiting for my husband to realize that I am the one that will be standing right here; waiting for my true love. My king made my dreams come true all because of your love. I promise there is nothing I would not do to preserve my love for you. I never thought this could happen to me, but it did. Tears keep falling from my face and soon my smile will fade into the still night."

I stopped reading and scanned her diary; reading only excerpts from it. Words and thoughts started filling my mind. "Wow, what is this failing marriage about? Who are these people that I am reading about and how did it end up on my balcony?" I took a deep breath and returned to the last page I had been reading, to continue the drama.

12/3/2014. 12:49 P.M.

"I can't sleep... I need to stay in prayer. So, I got up and prepared my Christmas cards for the upcoming company luncheon. I wanted to write something special to each employee and found that as I went on, I was the one receiving a message. Each person has a part in my life but I now have the pieces of my puzzle. I have labeled them, thanked them and I must recognize them and not forget them!

First was Patricia. She had a peaceful nature; calm and with a smile. Shalonda, my encourager, was the one that said, 'We can fix it'. Michelle's laughter helps me enjoy life. Lee is the hard worker, with a blend of perseverance, dedication and loyalty. Chris is intelligent, academically gifted, youthful, and has a zest for life. Nancy is my diffuser! She's always in the background, working getting things done without having to be in the spotlight. Mary is my "plan ahead person" who says, "Don't stay stuck in "today" there's tomorrow... and there's the Bahamas!" The day only has 24 hours. Becky helped me find strength when I thought I didn't have any! She is the one who always says, "Don't give up there's more!" And Linda made me believe my own words of faith and realization that God is there. She was my spiritual encouragement.

Then I realized that God was talking to me. While preparing my Christmas cards, I was writing or dictating to each of these wonderful people. It hit me. This is my message! God is HERE! I must not give in!! Be a fighter. It's not over. I am strong. I can do it. So, God does hear me.

12/16/2014. 5:01 A.M.

I realized Albert was absent, so became sad and cried again. Why do the tears never stop? Remember, dig deeper, there is joy. There is love. There is laugher. There is dancing. I need to dance. I need to feel alive. I need to feel pretty. Wait... I am alive and I am pretty. Just not right now.

Maybe sad is a part of the puzzle, but I guess overcome is too. Repair is, too. Darn, this puzzle keeps getting more pieces! Essential ingredients include one "C.G." A 'Calgon Take Me Away' person does not need to be real.

Make yourself feel good about you. Feel good and look good. Feel sexually confident, attractive, young, and feel HOT. Dress in a nice dress. Feel like the commercial. Feel good enough to tear off your blouse. Put a lacy bra on. Be prepared to reveal you and feel good. So have your 'Calgon Take Me Away' moments. Rest, relax, and indulge yourself to feel good."

✣ ✣ ✣ ✣ ✣ ✣ ✣ ✣

12/23/2014. 3:36 P.M.

"The sacrificial ham! How difficult can it be to cut up a spiral cut ham and put it on an aluminum sheet pan and take it to a luncheon? Well, today is the day it required many degrees of difficulty. First of all, I didn't do it last night. I did not feel like it. So this morning HE is saying, 'You didn't cut up the ham last night for the luncheon.'

Like, 'Oh my God.' I didn't know that I didn't do something I normally do!! So that's HIS shocker #1. The next shocker is that I tell him to do it. I surprised myself. Normally, I would have just done it myself. I would have said 'Okay' and gotten right on it. No, not this time. It took so much strength not to do it myself. Instead, I went and got ready for work.

'Yay for me,' I thought to myself. I am strong. I told him to do something and didn't take it back. It was a groundbreaking moment for me. I wanted to shout, 'YES!'

But then HE throws my moment of glee into the fire. 'I don't know what to do; I don't know how you can cut it and put it in the pan.'

Oh, no. He didn't just push my anger button, did he? I was trying so hard not to get angry, but of course I needed to see the "ugly ham". I wanted to fix it, but instead I used my "angry" voice and told him to do it.

"But I don't know how," he said.

"How could you not know how? You separate one layer at

a time, trim off the fat with a slight overlay of ham slices over the other layers," I retorted. Oh my God, I have O.C.D., so I couldn't let an ugly tray leave my house. It is all about presentation! And he knows that, but still I refused to fix it. "Just go ahead and fix it."

Then he got brave very brave. Albert was not going to fix it. Instead, he knew how to move my strings like a puppet. He was manipulative, although I never noticed before. "No, you need to fix it," he refused to comply. These were the wrong words to tell me.

I lost it. "Fix it? You want me to fix it like everything else YOU messed up this past year?" Then I saw it so clear. Albert was controlling me to fix it. He messed things up and I fixed them. But no... not this time. I was dying inside to do it, but I caved in to fix the ham for the cause.

Then I just walked away, back to dressing up for work. In my head, I thought about ugly tray of ham. Then an inner voice said, 'Who cares what the ham looks like?'

The truth is, I care.

And yay for me; I guess no one complained about the yucky ham. Today, I realized so many things because of the ham. Who would have thought I could learn so much about myself all before going into work?"

8/11/2015. 12:01 A.M.

"We have been apart for a year, but living in the same house. I don't know why. I haven't found a good enough answer. I just have good excuses. We finally started speaking to each other, but it is so superficial. Nothing gets resolved or concluded. It always turns into a fight and it's always my fault.

9/12/2015. 5:26 A.M.

I started to write things down because I am so devastated. I am so low, yet some days confident. When I tell someone my stories, I laugh and cry; I can't believe myself. I didn't realize I had O.C.D. about so many things. I am so angry at Albert. I speak through grinded, low, locked voice to keep from yelling. My anger sometimes scares me. My mind is constantly running, thinking, planning, fixing – or trying to understand – praying. Trying to find logic. Seeking answers to the past and trying to see the future. I know there is a future, but I guess the question is, 'What am I going to do?'

Well, I am always making decisions for my job. That is how I make a living, by making decisions. But my own personal life, I suck at it. I just don't follow through with the decisions about my own personal circumstances.

9/20/2015. 3:03 P.M.

I, KIKI. What does Kiki want to do with the marriage and her living arrangement? See, I just went into third person. Another realization about me is that I am the "Do it" police. I often ask, "Did you do this, or did you do that?" It fell on deaf ears.

Albert certainly knew how to push the anger button on me. For example, if he said, "What did you say?"

And I replied, "You heard me, didn't you?"

He'd say, "No, repeat it."

Oh no, not another control phase. No! I am not repeating anything anymore, ever. It was like he wanted to see my angry side. It was a form of attention, rather than silence or being ignored altogether.

9/28/2015. 8:16 A.M.

Albert now lives in another room of the house, but he won't leave. Why should he? I am fixing the mess and paying for everything. I leave him alone. He has a home, cable, car, food, cell phone, and no worries, no budget, no bill paying worries.

10/8/2015. 6:16 P.M.

Romance oozes when he speaks (yeah right). He is unsympathetic to any pain I may be feeling, emotionally or otherwise. Like, my filling came out from my back molar and it was so painful, but when Albert saw my expression all he could say was, "What did you do now?"

Not, "Are you okay? Is something the matter? Do you need me to do something for you?" Or anything compassionate. All I want is care and affection, is that too much to ask? Maybe it is for me – from him – in this relationship? If you can call it that anymore."

10/11/2015. 12:16 A.M.

"Today I feel free and good. I am going to watch a movie while Albert sleeps. It's 12:20 A.M. now, but I am not sleepy yet. I had a great session today with Mrs. Cotton. I think this is going to help me in so many ways. Afterwards, I went to a field that laid at. It wasn't pretty or nice at all. I couldn't believe I was there. Today I told Albert that I didn't want to hear any mean comments.

11/1/2015. 3:25 P.M.

It felt good reading what the doctor said about me during this past October mental assessment. Well, New Years is coming. Let's see what happens."

11/2/2015. 10:10 A.M.

Albert admitted 'she ignored me' these past few days. Probably upset over nothing as usual.

I couldn't believe it, but he did say it to me. After all that has happened, my husband still feels distant to me. Sometimes I feel like giving up and moving on, but that is the wrong thing to do. Well I don't know where I will end up this New Years, but it might be with my friends. He's almost home from work. We will see what happens on that day. Remember, no drinking. Yeah, right. Can't believe it came down to that.

11/5/2015. 9:05 P.M.

Life has to get better. I made a CD of 90's music and some uplifting songs. I really needed to that."

11/6/2015. 8:16 P.M.

"Just woke up from a three hour nap after work. I was sleepy from staying up last night. We had a beer. Actually, two, but it was cool just relaxing here at home. Tomorrow we go see Doctor Cotton together. That should be interesting. I hope it goes well. Let's see what he has to say about me to her. I am little hungry and don't want to cook. I guess I'll cook something really fast. Work was so boring. I kept trying to fall asleep while being there. My boss was out sick and the other assistant took the whole week off."

11/7/2015. 2:22 P.M.

"Today is an ugly day. I am so upset. I hate arguing over nothing. I am hungry, but I want to go to church. It's been half a year or more since I've gone. That's not good at all. Here I go mad. Well last night, we went out to some club. It was so boring. I had an awesome earlier day with my friend, she's a blast. I need

to hang out with her more often."

11/10/2015. 6:01 A.M.

"I was just choking on cheerios. I think we are staying in tonight. Albert says he's feeling sick. Like maybe he has the flu or something. He just wants too much attention; like over the top! He needs to cry, I guess."

11/14/2015. 4:21 P.M

"Today was an awesome day. I had a dance practice. Then it was lunch with some of my friends. I wish I could go out with my friends without Albert all the time. Just to get away and hang out with them."

12/31/2015. 4:00 A.M.

"Last day of the year is today. I do hope this next year is a great year.

After I finished reading this diary, I thought, *"This poor Kiki needs to get a divorce and stay far away from her husband Albert. How is he keeping up? Why does he not want any help?"*

So many questions came into my head. I wondered, who was Kiki and how did the diary get into my apartment? The mystery puzzled me. Could I be Kiki? Is this why I was wearing woman's clothes and a blonde wing?

At that point, I determined that a professional therapist would be the next step for me. I wanted to talk about Momo and other things I had experienced that did not make total sense to me. Was I going crazy or did I have a split personality? Did mental illness run in my family's genes? I did not remember any of my family members being crazy or lost in their mind.

"What is wrong with me? I am so scared right now..."

Chapter Twelve

BETRAYAL, LIES AND A PLAN

Bert started talking about going back to his hometown for Christmas to see his family, but without me. I did not know what to think or what he was really up to. I just knew we needed some space for ourselves.

With that in mind, I told him I was okay with it. He was only supposed to be gone for two weeks, however, after prying on his social media accounts; I found out that Bert had been seeing another twink. It was a skinny, 24-year old of about 120 lbs., 5'9" and short, blonde hair and blue eyes. This guy named David was someone Bert met while in his hometown; who was now his boyfriend. I wanted to reach out to David and bust Bert for cheating on me. Instead, I kept my cool and did not let him know I knew about this new discovery.

The calls were not consistent anymore. At times, I would talk to him days apart and for only minutes each time. After a month, we completely stopped talking. I started moving on with my life as a single man. It was terribly tough, because I was dealing with so many different emotions about my inner demons. I was falling apart all around, from my personality to mental aptitude. Some mornings I was so depressed that I did not want to get out of my bed. My mind tortured me with good memories and then several bad ones.

At times, I missed Bert. I knew it would take time to get past the mourning period of being without him. It just felt like it happened so quickly – and without any preparation. It was like being abandoned.

After two months, Bert ended up coming back to me. I did not even contemplate whether or not to give him a second chance. Truthfully, I loved him. I wanted to give our love another opportunity to flourish.

However, Bert came back a changed man. Things felt different now with him. He was very secretive about certain things, especially his cell phone. My roommate did not want him living with us in the apartment, because it was too small. It was only a one bedroom place. Although she didn't really want me to move, we both knew that having three people in a one bedroom apartment would not work.

So, Bert and I moved into a mutual older friend's house named Ana. Ana was like a flip-flop, which meant that she flip-flopped sides in friendship quite a lot. Ana was 31 years old and had been married and divorced in the same calendar year. She had light brown, wavy hair with blond highlights that hung past her shoulders. Her green eyes complemented her fair skin tone and freckles on her face. Ana was a girly girl that loved decorating her home in pink; everywhere. She enrolled in basic study courses to get her Associates Degree at a nearby college, so most days she was out of the house. Ana had lots of space in her three bedroom house. She had been my friend for a couple of years. She met Bert and instantly had a connection with him.

Soon they became really close. I thought it was a little strange but did not give it much more thought. They even talked a lot like mother and son conversations. She did not do that with me, but I guess they had their own connection. The mother hen role was a stretch, but Bert thrived on that bond. He must have missed having his mom around.

Three years was a long time of being in a back and forth relationship. I continued to stay with Bert because I just wanted somebody to love me. I knew he really did love me, although he had made a mistake. I overlooked it, but in time, my love started to fade away. It was mainly because Bert could not give me the answers as to why he did not come back after two weeks and why he was with another man besides me. Whenever I asked, his answer was always the same. "I do not know". With all the cheating, misleading and distrust between us, Bert was never truly honest with me about anything.

Deep down in my gut, I knew that Bert also continued

to do me wrong while I was gone to work. By now, I was working at a Mexican restaurant as a server and still performing for different club events occasionally. Basically, I supported both of us with two jobs, while he stayed home and most likely cheated on me. Unfortunately, I could not prove it and Ana told me he was not doing any wrong that she knew of. We would get into arguments when I questioned him about the possibility of him cheating on me again.

"You know, once a cheater, always a cheater," I'd sometimes say to Bert. Could I trust my good, dear friend Ana and my boyfriend both not to lie to my face? I had to, since I had no other choice and no proof.

Bert got upset at me for stupid reasons. I left for a while to get out of our place, so he hid things on his cell phone or in the apartment. My clothes often got ripped up and thrown away. I said all kinds of mean things to me. He hit me all the time and I let him. I knew our relationship would not last much longer. He started having crazy outbursts and actions around me.

Most of the time, I was fucked up on some drugs – or popping pills mixed with alcohol – while I was with him. I wanted out of the messed up relationship with Bert. It had become way too toxic and I was losing myself to drugs, too.

What to do? How could I break free from him? Who would help me? What was the ultimate plan for him to return back to his home town city of Seguin? I had many questions, but knew it was not going to be easy for me to break up with

Bert. He was not going to let me go without a vindictive fight, either.

When I finally reached a conclusion to end things, I thought to myself, *'So here it goes... all or nothing.'* I did not want Bert anymore and knew that I must move on without him. I decided to ask Ana for help.

"Ana, please. Who else can help me get out of this toxic relationship?" I asked her privately one day.

She thought for a minute. "What about Nicole?"

Nicole was our mutual friend. She had been born in Mexico, but had moved to San Antonio five years ago. She got married a couple of years later, but her husband of two years left her within three months of living in the U.S. She was an unhappy girl that did not make friends easily. She had a chip on her shoulder and because of her attitude; people simply didn't enjoy her company. Nicole was 28 years old, 5'6" and 162 lbs., with jet black, short, thin hair, and eye glasses that made it difficult to see her black eyes. She always seemed to be wearing loose-fitting, black clothing. That did not work well for her. Nicole lived with some guy that she barely knew.

We all made up a plan. I did not know how to tell Bert I did not love him. So I went to the girls and told them, "I don't want to be with him anymore. I do not want him to know that I do not love him, but I do not know how to break up with him without him going crazy."

Deep down, I knew Bert was going to hit me if I told him to his face. He always had expressed a fear of me getting away or of someone else taking me away from him. "Please girls, will you please help me?"

We talked about it for months. I told them I didn't know how to handle the situation. They offered suggestions on how to break up with him and tell him. I knew that even if I was honest with him, he was going to attack me. He would go ballistic, because Bert was still in love with me. It took months and months of preparation – with many different plots – how to get him to go back to Seguin. It was just a matter of how and when to do it without him going insane and taking it out on me.

"What if you get him to sleep with another guy?" suggested Ana and Nicole. "Maybe Bert will want the other guy more than you and leave with him?"

"Possibly. I know some guys that like him a lot and want to be in a relationship with him," I replied. "I know he wants them too, but he didn't do anything with them because I know them." It was true; Bert kept his cheating on the down low and made sure I did not ever find out, or so he thought.

"What if we make up a person?" suggested Ana.

"Yeah, like a fake profile!" Nicole chimed in.

"Hmmm. It might work..." I thought out loud.

So the girls set up a fake profile for a guy named Charles. He was a black, muscular firefighter in his thirties. He was tall, dark and a very handsome man. The girls even found a picture of some model from New York to use for the profile picture. In his "*About Me*" section, it stated that he lived in Seguin. We added simple, basic information about him and only one picture. It was all a plot to try to lure Bert back to his hometown. The "*mouse and cheese*" plan.

Once the fake profile was ready, we tried to befriend Bert twice, but he did not accept it. I wanted to get him to fall in love with this fake person so that he would want to leave me again. It was supposed to work, but Bert did not take the bait. I wondered, why?

Then, the girls got really creative. They started having that fake profile Charles send me messages on Facebook, as though we were having a relationship. They had so much fun taking turns texting me as this fake person. I responded, going along with their plan, but I felt like it was a stupid idea.

The fourth plan was mine. I was still performing and hanging out with a male dancer named Rico, from one of our shows called '*Drag Stardom*'. Rico was a Latin heartthrob, playboy type of guy. I did not like him because I knew it was all a game to him. He was 6' ft. tall with a light skin tone, 165 lbs. of shapely muscle, hazel brown eyes and short, brown hair. Rico was indeed a beautiful guy.

I told the girls, "I am going to pretend I am performing at our last contest for the season. It is really important that I win this competition to continue being part of the new cast in the show coming up next month. I am going by myself."

Actually, there was no final show contest. It was all a lie. I was not even performing that night. I was actually going to go out and have some fun with friends. I was going to flirt with Rico and take pictures with him, just to give the illusion that something happened between us that night.

So later that night, I put the plan in place. I told Bert, "I have to perform tonight for the last contest show of the season. I'll be performing with our friend Rico."

"You never mentioned this before," replied Bert.

"Rico is going to being picking me up and some other contestants. We are all riding together in that small SUV," I explained.

Bert instantly wanted to go with me. "Sorry, there is not going to be room for you."

"Well, can you ask them?"

"Sure," I said, fully knowing I would not. After I pretended to call them, I reported back. "He told me he did not have enough space to bring another person."

Bert looked pissed. I left that night with my performance luggage in hand.

I did what I said I would do. I flirted with Rico and had a random person take pictures of us both eating at a restaurant together. I took one of just the two of us sitting next to each other closely at the club. I asked Rico to post them on Facebook and tag me in them.

Then, I 'accidently' left my cell phone behind at the house. Bert must have seen my cell phone, and like I knew he would, he started going through it. Ana was still up with one of her guy pals, Tino who happened to be there while Bert was doing this. Tino was 25 years old; a stalky guy of 240 lbs. He was 6'1" tall, Hispanic, kept a shaved head that was glossy when his tank skin perspired. He wasn't much of a talker; just drinker. Tino was always drunk whenever I was around him.

When I got home, Bert started yelling and screaming at me. I was caught off-guard because I didn't know he had gone through my phone. I went into a defensive mode. '*How should I handle this?*' I thought to myself. '*This is what I wanted, but shit, not all at once.*' It was suddenly so overwhelming for me. I felt guilty, as though I really did cheat, but I knew I had not. It was all made up lies and secretive plans.

Bert was so upset. He had thrown my clothes all over the bedroom and pictures were torn. He had thrown food on the walls. It was crazy. I had no control of the situation. He was so beyond mad. He was outraged with me. I told him to try to calm down so we could talk about this. He was foaming from the mouth, with saliva flying everywhere. He was spitting while he was talking. I had never seen him like that, ever. I crossed the line of no return.

He said, "You like fucking around on me? You have another dude named Charles lined up, texting him about wanting to leave me for him in Seguin. You think he's better than me? Fine, we will see at the end who is better! You are messing around even tonight with Rico while you are supposed to be competing for what, someone else's dick? You are a fucking asshole. You fucked with the wrong person." Then, he threw my cell phone. I picked it up right away and kept it in my hands.

Meanwhile, Ana and her friend Tino tried to get Bert to calm down. None of us could. They stood back and watched everything unraveling. I kept looking at Ana because both of us knew what I did was all a lie; we had both made it all up together. I tried to speak to Bert in a calm voice. "Look it is not been working out for a good while now. I do not want Rico or Charles, and I do not want to hurt you. I just cannot do this with you anymore. Go home to your family and friends in Seguin where you are obviously happier than staying here with me."

Bert said, "Who do you think you are fooling? Fuck you! Now you are worried about my wellbeing. Fuck you thinking that you know what is best for me." Bert started to pull his things out of the closet in our bedroom. "I am leaving, but I'm taking you down. When I am done with you, no one will ever want you around. Your reputation will be so messed up! Just wait, mother fucker."

I lost it after hearing all that. He knew I was working with so many different charities and child abuse prevention, too. All while getting my name out to the world. He was not going to take me out like that. "Get the hell out!" I yelled. "Leave now and you better not spread lies about me." I followed Bert around the room while we both screamed at each other. Ana and Tino kept a distance away. I noticed them in the background every so often.

My cell phone was still in my hand when he got to the door. I started to close the door behind him. Bert turned and started pushing the door back open. I quickly reacted to push the door closed and ended up accidentally hitting his ear. I managed to lock the door. Standing with my back to the door, I heard the car turn on and Bert leaving. I told Ana and Tino, "I am going to sleep. He should not come back tonight."

I went to my room and changed into some shorts and a T-shirt. One hour later, I heard his voice outside of the house. I ran to the window to see. Yeah, it was Bert, but he had the house phone instead of his cell phone. I ran to where the phone was supposed to be. Sure enough, the home phone was missing from its stand. I should have unplugged it in, but I was not thinking. I ran to wake up Ana and Tino. Neither of them was in the house. I was fucked; I heard him talking to the police. I feared he was claiming I attacked him. Shit, I was going down, just like he said.

I ran to look for my cell phone to call my family for help. It was on the kitchen counter. I did not remember leaving it there. It was missing the battery. Bert must have come in and took it apart while he got the home phone.

As I stood looking at my phone, wondering what to do, I heard the door open. I ran to it. It was Ana's friend Tino, coming in. I asked him where Ana was. He pointed outside. I saw Ana talking to Bert. I went outside to see what was going on. She was on my side. I yelled across the yard, "Ana did you hear? Bert called the cops saying I beat him up."

I looked at Bert and said, "That is bullshit, I have witnesses. Both Ana and Tino."

He looked at me with a smug smirked and said, "No. You got it all backwards. They are my witnesses against you, stupid. You were played like a fool, sucker."

I turned to Ana with a shocked expression. She said nothing. I told him, "She is lying to you. Ana was the one who helped me make up all those things. I did not cheat on you; I just could not be with you anymore."

We started arguing again. He came at me. I pushed him away. Then Ana came at me and grabbed me. I pushed her too. Then Tino came at me, swinging, defending his friend Ana. I was now being attacked by all three of them. I remember biting Ana on the arm. I was defending myself, while swinging, kicking and hitting whomever I could. I was fighting them from all different directions. Then I jumped on Tino. I was no match against this big dude, so I bit him somewhere on his back. He grabbed me by my T-shirt and swung me off him, flying through the air. My body smashed hard against the concrete floor.

I must have blacked out. I didn't remember anything between the biting and hitting, until I woke up in a cold, dirty, old jail cell alone; all bruised and bloody. I could not move my left arm. The ultimate plan backfired on me, after all. I was framed by my friends and the ones I trusted. How did I let this happen to me?

A couple of days later, I still sat in the jail cell. A lawyer, Mr. Reynolds, came to see me. This 50+ year-old man sat across the table from me. His slim body looked very professional in a grey suit. A wooden walking cane accentuated his short gray hair, giving the impression he had spent many years walking these halls. He said, "Charges have been filed against you. I am your court-appointed lawyer for this case. The other three all had the same story painted of you as a druggie and alcoholic that had way too much to drink and went crazy on them all. They said you viciously attacked and bit all of them."

"No, no, Mr. Reynolds... this is what really happened..." Whereupon, I told my lawyer the real story; my side of the story. Mr. Reynolds seemed like he genuinely believed me. I knew I was just a case to him. At the end of the day, he didn't care any less about me.

"Okay. You will see the judge in a couple of weeks. Stay positive and we'll see how this plays out," he instructed.

A month later, I appeared in front of Judge Peterson. He was a tough, Asian man with a reputation for being a hard ass. I discovered that Bert, Ana and Tino had all dropped the charges, but the State had to pick it up anyways. Luckily, the Judge read the case over thoroughly and stated in court that; "*This was a breakup gone wrong.*"

Furthermore, he believed I was defending myself against three people and since their stories were too neat, it was clear they were lying and covering up for each other. The police wrote in their report that all three must have all been holding me down; each taking turns punching and kicking me. They arrived at this conclusion from the blood and bruises all over my body. These were visible evidence the police had photographed. The pictures were shown in the court room. Turns out, I was the victim of that attack, while being unconscious. They did not even give me the opportunity of fair terms to fight back. He dismissed my case and told me to stay out of trouble.

I was a free man. Later that day, I was finally released back into the public.

Chapter Thirteen

FINAL SILENCE

The dark night was still as I looked up at a full moon in the sky. It was almost 2:00 a.m. I stood outside the front of my apartment, looking at nature all around me. But something didn't feel right. I couldn't put my finger on it.

A car drove around the complex a couple of times. It was a blue dodge with black rims and dark, tinted windows. For some reason, I followed it with my eyes every time it passed. I never moved a step. Then the car stopped a distance away, where it remained parked and idled for a couple of minutes. This time, I saw more people outside. They were just coming and going from the complex. I decided to walk to our mailbox and check today's mail, since I had forgotten about it earlier.

As I started walking, I heard someone from behind me

call out, "Kiki!" I turned around to find a fist suddenly slam into my face. It ripped my lips into pieces and blood gushed out. I was knocked down to the ground. I had no chance to defend myself.

I laid there on the cold cement ground, with blood gushing out. Then I heard, "Finish him," from a distance. Three gunshots went off. Bullets hit various parts of my body, one after the other. I felt them pierce through my body. I laid there frightened, powerless and unable to move.

"Help!" I screamed out, crying for help. But no one came to my rescue. I heard screeching tires and then I saw the car racing away. Was I going to die? Am I dying? Who did this to me and why?

Chaos ensued. I heard people screaming and crying. Then I heard police and ambulances arriving. I just lay there, looking at the mystical, full moon. I said my prayers to God because I did not know if I would make it out of this. Then, my body gave out.

I heard a voice near my head. "Penny Juku put a hit on you," Momo whispered in my ear. "She made Kiki steal money from those drug dealers, instead of sleeping with them. Kiki took their stash of almost $4,000 and ran home. They followed her and beat the shit out of her. They almost killed her, but instead, she agreed to become their personal property if they let her live. They left her at that building... remember when you wore that dress?"

I was so confused. Momo said, "Kris you are also Kiki. Well, Kiki she messed herself up bad because that next day she called one of those guys and told them she was going to tell the cops. That was a couple of days ago. You were set up and Kiki was the bait to get rid of you. Penny Juku wants you dead so badly that she is willing to sacrifice her own life too, just to get rid of you. She has gone mad and there is no stopping her or keeping you alive anymore. Our game is over. No one can help us now. None of us are safe around Penny Juku or you."

I heard doctors talking, but I could not understand what they were saying. Their voices were too far away. I could not even open my eyes. *Why wouldn't my eyes open? Was I dreaming? What is going on with me?*

The doctors got closer and I heard them clearly. One doctor said, "They really did a number on him. Poor guy. He was so young. We stopped his internal bleeding, but he lost so much blood. Does he have any family or visitors waiting outside for him, so we can give them an update?"

Another doctor responded, "No there is no one waiting for him. Time will tell if he makes it out of here alive."

Then, the heart machine I was hooked up to reveals no heart activity. I flat-lined and then the monotonous tone filled the room with silence. With it, Kris left and took all the others, too... Momo, Michael, Israeli, Miguel, Penny Juku, and Kiki.

Finally, it was quiet; total silence all around. The voices all stopped. The voices were collectively all finally DEAD.

About the Author

DIVON DELGADO

Divon Delgado was born and raised in San Antonio, Texas. His natural, creative talents have given him numerous opportunities, as an actor, model, composer and five times published author. He has performed voiceovers and developed a reputation as a notable humanitarian and child abuse awareness advocate. Ever the entrepreneur, Divon Delgado is also the creator of a fragrance collection called "Sexy Back" and "Besame Bebe", which can be found at: www.divonville.com. His first book received recognition and an acknowledgement letter from The White House; signed by President Obama and First Lady Michelle.

Although Divon does have a degree in accounting diploma and has studied in the Psychology sector, one of his primary passions is in participating and giving back to his community of San Antonio, Texas, where he resides. Divon also does pro bono work for individuals in need of counseling.

Prior to these most recent pursuits, Divon worked as a "Court Appointed Special Advocate" volunteer for the National

C.A.S.A association. While there, he participated in the judicial system hands-on as a liaison between the families, protective custody services and the children. By working closely with the dedicated staff at DFPS – Texas Child Protective Services (CPS) – Divon has been able to continue his efforts to preserve the wellbeing of children involved in distressing situations.

Divon Delgado has spoken live at the Valero Energy Corporation, The Salvation Army Hope Center, and many other companies to interact with victims for encouragement. He is always ready to share his story and experiences; to educate listeners about the taboo topic of abuse. Public speaking has given Divon the desire to reach a broader audience; hence, he has been traveling and doing lectures and book readings on this topic.

Divon was also the 2014-2015 Media Chair with JDRF, a non-profit organization in search of a cure for Diabetes. His team – "Divon's Advocates" – walked and ran 5k for the cause. Most recently, Divon has been working as a "Child Specialist" for a TX non-profit agency. Children understand the difference between those who work their case vs. those who care about their wellbeing and future.

Visit DivonVille.com to reach author Divon Delgado and find him at the next book signing, film, TV show, music video or TV commercial. Most of all, Divon thanks his fans for their support with his creative aspirations. You can also possibly find him doing a lecture at his bookstore in San Antonio, Texas, located at 6412 Bandera Road.

www.ingramcontent.com/pod-product-compliance
Lightning Source LLC
Chambersburg PA
CBHW051835020726
47502CB00005B/1793
9780692761281